When Life Shatters

Johnny B

Dedication

I dedicate this book to all the Doctors, Nurses and staff for the six months that I spent in Bristol's Frenchay and Taunton's Musgrove Park hospitals, also Alfred Morris Rehabilitation Centre within Musgrove Park Hospital grounds. Without their help I wouldn't have been able to write this book, God bless you all.

Chapter 1

Johnny B, a guitar vocalist, with two good friends and an electronic drum machine. Steve on Bass and Andy on guitar and vocals, had been gigging, together for a while. They played all over the South west, Bristol, Bath, Exeter, Taunton, and Bridgwater. Playing at local pubs and clubs. They met each other at different gigs. That was, until the night it all changed for John.

John pulled up outside his house, after another successful gig. He unloaded the van as usual and carried the equipment into the house to store it under the stairs. John was still high on excitement and the thrill of performing in front of people. He couldn't sleep just yet, he locked the van up, locked the front door and then went to the fridge and grabbed a bottle of beer, sat down in the sitting room, and took a couple of mouthfuls.

He thought about the night's performance. Well, they were dancing that's a good sign he thought. He started to unwind sipping his beer and starting to feel tired. Right, he said to him self. I'm up early tomorrow for work. He headed upstairs to check on the boys, picking up a few toys on the floor as he went. John quietly opened their bedroom door. The light shone in from the hall and into their room. He pushed the door open further, placed the toys quietly in the toy box and walked to the end of the bunk beds. Jason who was 6 years old and Bradley who was 3 years old were sleeping peacefully. John grinned to himself thinking how lucky he was to have two great kids. He moved the hair from Jason's face; it felt so silky under his rough hand. He saw their cat Willow curled up soundly for the night at the foot of Jason's bed. John carefully pulled the blankets back over Jason's shoulder and kissed them both on the forehead and said to himself good night boys. He went back downstairs to unwind in his chair and finish his beer. He loosened his tie with one hand and took a swig of his beer with the other. Looking over to the corner of the room where he kept six Koi Carp in a deep tank, the biggest was nearly 8 inches long. He smiled watching them swim, leaving him feeling calm and peaceful. Time for bed he thought, finishing his beer. He checked the front door was locked and he headed up stairs to finally get some sleep. He checked on the boys once again. His wife Gina slept soundly most nights. She had the blankets drawn around her shoulder, one hand under the pillow and one Foot poking out of the blankets. She said she couldn't sleep if her feet were all tucked in, and in all the years John had known her; she has always slept this way.

As he undone his buttons on his shirt took it off and hung it over the chair, He couldn't help remembering when the boys would get sick with a cold or flu and no medicine would help them, except the medicine of mom and dad's hugs and kisses.

Gina and John would take turns seeing if they were sleeping, putting their heads around the door just letting enough light through to make sure they were sleeping soundly. This, sadly, was the only thing Gina and John had in common anymore. When John would go and check on them, He would sometimes sing a lullaby to them until they fell back to sleep. He loved to watch them fall asleep and just experience the contentment he felt as a father, but he also loved to see how peaceful they looked. The next time it would be Gina's turn. She would get into bed with one of them usually the youngest Bradley, snuggle him into her bosom, and there in the comfort of his mother's arms he would fall sound asleep, forgetting all the aches and pains of the day.

John lifted the quilt back carefully and slipped into bed. He eased himself down on to the mattress so as not to a wake Gina. This was his routine every night of the week. Park up the van and unload the gear and slip quietly into bed. Gina would always be in bed before he got home. She wouldn't let him touch her all the closeness had gone along time ago. They didn't have a sex life anymore; they hardly had a life at all. They had become two people who lived together supporting the two

Boys'. Gina was always out with her friends or working late. Quite simply, they had grown apart. They both still wanted the boys to have a family who lived together. It may seem strange, but Gina and John worked it out over time and the boys were happy. That's all that ever mattered to John. There was no pleasing Gina for anything in the last 2 or 3 years everything that went wrong always seemed to be John's fault. No matter what it was, things that happened at the boys' school, or what happened to her at work, it all boiled down to some how being John's fault. He just lived with it. What else was he supposed to do?

Chapter 2

John tried to get comfortable in bed rolling over one side then the other. He didn't want to hear Gina complain about that too. It wasn't long before the sweet surrender of sleep came over him. John dreamt of a time when he was a boy, his family and John would visit Nan and Grandad. They would drive up to their house on a Sunday afternoon. They didn't live too far away from us. All the windows would be open in the old Vauxhall Victor as it took off down the winding road, the smoke pluming out behind the car like grey swirling tornados of smoke and air. John's sister's long brown hair would be blowing in the wind and as his Father would sing some old 60's songs, His Mother would hum along in the background. The drive wasn't to long, but they enjoyed there time together. Before long they could see their house in the distance.

John loved visiting Nan and Grandad. They could roam through the fields, and his brother Mark and John would climb on an old, dilapidated tractor and pretend they were farmers turning up the soil for planting. John's sister would laugh at them from her spot in the field of wildflowers where she would read her book of short romantic stories.

Their house was old but cosey. It was all built by his Grandad a long time ago, they had gas central heating put in awhile back. Making the whole house lovely and warm The winter months were cosey they kept the fireplace open, and Christmas time, they would light the fire, it really made Christmas special. When John and his family went to visit them, to give them there presents, they would sit by the fire, there face's glowed from the heat.

As John's dad parked the car, all three of them, John's older sister Christine, and his younger brother Mark and John would race up to the big farmhouse to try to be the first one to open the door. They would race past Grandad screaming there 'hellos' to him. He would tell them to slow down, as they all scrambled for the door. John's parents would bring stuff in from the car. Nan would hug all three kids one at a time and ask who was ready for Homemade bread just out the oven.

John awoke from his dream just as he was going to bite into Nan's warm bread.
He had to go to the loo. He got up, went to the bathroom and on his return, he felt a piercing pain in his head and immediately his field of vision was blurry, He felt like he had been on a roller

coaster a million times. His stomach turned one-way, and his head swirled around until he was dizzy. There was a shooting pain across his forehead as he stumbled forward to reach for the banister.

That was the last coherent thought he would have in over three months. He had reached for the banister but missed and toppled down the stairs. His body shot from one side of the stairs to the other, heaving his 6-foot tall and 12 and a half Stone body at lightning speed to the bottom. The thick carpet muffled most of his fall. The left shoulder was seared with pain, as the bone sliced its way through the skin and protruded outward at a weird angle. Above his right eye was a large swelling slowly darkening as the bruise pushed its way through to the surface, where his head had struck the wall with a loud and forceful thump. Slumped in a battered heap at the bottom of the stair's, He was conscious enough to drag his bruised and battered body towards the sofa in the sitting room slowly dragging his arm behind him, He crawled on all fours to the sitting room sofa where he had, an hour earlier, sat sipping his beer, now, unknowingly with his head pounding as if a grenade had gone off in it.

Gina was startled when she thought she heard a loud thump. She lay still for a few minutes, rubbed the sleep out of her eyes and waited to hear if there was any other noise or if she had just imagined it. She felt John's side of the bed. He wasn't there. After a few more minutes and still in her sleepy state, Gina got out from under the quilt, sat up on the side of the bed and slipped her feet into her slippers that were right at her feet. She thought she should go and investigate what the noise was or if there was even a noise at all. Gina checked the boy's room first. They were both sound asleep. Willow the cat was fast asleep; the noise hadn't awakened any of them. Maybe she had just imagined the noise she though as she closed their door and headed for the stairs. She switched on the light on at the bottom of the stairs. She walked towards the sitting room, following her instincts. As she passed a small table in the hallway her fingers ran across the smooth marble tabletop and quickly rearranged a small daisy that was out of place in the flower arrangement. Gina hadn't seen anything that seemed out of place. She came to the sitting room and reached around the corner with her hand and switched on a small table lamp. She saw John's legs poking out from around the arm of the sofa. He didn't move when she called his name. She knew John tended to fall asleep on the sofa and then come up to bed later, which was good enough for her. Gina didn't like sharing her bed with her husband anymore anyway. She assumed it had been John who had made the noise, and without investigating any further, turned out the light and went back upstairs to bed. She was furious at him for waking her up. 'He's lucky he didn't wake the boys' she thought as she walked back up the stairs to her room. John lay on the sofa, the blood slowly streamed from the gaping hole on John's left shoulder where the bone had pierced the skin. The blood trickled down the sofa and onto the carpet, John's breath was laboured and shallow, He lay there barely alive. The odd flicker of a foot or his hand, that was it.

Chapter 3

◆◆ ● ◆◆

G ina was usually the first one up in the house in the morning. Her work at the local newspaper demanded it, working all hours of the day and night, or so she made everyone believe. The announcer on the radio was talking about all the rain their area had been having for the last few days when the clock radio beside the bed awoke Gina at 6 am. She stretched and groaned under the quilt, she threw back the quilt and slipped her feet into her slippers and made her way to the bathroom. She noticed that John had still not come up to bed. This angered her because the sofa was being ruined by him sleeping on it, but that thought disappeared her mind as quickly as it entered, because the alternative of him sleeping in the bed wasn't what she wanted either. She could always buy another sofa she thought.

Gina closed the bathroom door and reached in behind the shower curtain and started the water for her morning shower. She also clicked on the shower radio that hung on the wall and sang along with K C and the Sunshine Band, Give it up. While the water was getting warm in the shower, she went to the sink and reached up to the medicine cabinet and brought out her toothbrush and toothpaste. The cold water ran slowly in the sink as the steam started to rise out above the shower curtain, gently inviting Gina to come into its warm embrace. She left her toothbrush and paste on the side of the sink and let her nightgown fall to the floor. The warm water cascaded over her shoulders as she thought of all the events of the day yet to come. There were a few appointments she had to reconfirm; there was the meeting with the editor of the newspaper at 1.30pm, and last but deliciously not least, was dinner with Lee at The Bistro Restaurant at 6 pm. With all the days' monotony filling her mind, Gina quickly washed her hair and got out of the shower.

Dressed in tight jeans and a white T shirt partly tucked in at the front, Gina made her way down the stairs. She spotted a dark maroon stain on the stair's carpet but dismissed it as something she would get John to clean up later.

They had their fights and issues over the work being done but when it was finally complete, they both adored it. It was some of John's best work he was such a perfectionist. Gina waited for the kettle to boil so she could have her first cup of tea. As she waited, she went from room to room opening the curtains to let in the first light of the day. Her mind still wandered and deliberated over the day's events to come. As she came into the sitting room, the front of the sofa faced away from her, so, to Gina, it looked like John was still sleeping, just as he was when she came to investigate the noise in the middle of the night. She was mad as hell that he was still laying there. 'Why does he insist on making me angry all the time' she wondered. "He should be up by now" she muttered under her breath as she came around the front of the sofa. Intending to shake John awake and send him directly upstairs, Gina stopped dead, the colour quickly draining from her face. There lay John, blood coagulated on his shoulder, and she looked at the large swelling on his forehead, the blood had trickled down onto the carpet. John's body had laid there over night, breath laboured, and life lingering in the balance.

Gina walked hesitantly toward John. She slowly extended her right foot towards his left foot and gave it a slight nudge. John let out a painful moan but did not move. Gina swallowed hard, like the lump in her throat was ten times too big to go down. She knew that she had no choice but to phone for an ambulance. Not out of concern for John, but rather to get this mess cleaned up before the boys were awake. "How dare he make me deal with something like this?' she thought in complete frustration. As she waited for the ambulance to arrive through the early morning calm, she paced through the kitchen. Within ten minutes the ambulance had arrived, and a Paramedic jumped out the back and hit the ground. The driver raced around to the back door, brought out the stretcher and filled it with all the equipment they would need to save John's life. Gina greeted them at the door and calmly told them "He's in the sitting room" and pointed them in his general direction. Without another thought, she then went upstairs to the boys' room to prepare them for the day at school. She had so much to get done today, and now this?

The Paramedic's worked feverishly to get John's body to respond. He was not responding to any treatment they gave him, but he was managing to still take very shallow breaths on his own. The Paramedic's placed John onto the stretcher, fastened the safety straps, and rushed out of the house and into the waiting ambulance. Once inside, they hooked John up to an intravenous, but he was still not responding to stimuli. They called ahead to the hospital and told the awaiting team that their patient's vital signs were low; there was a contusion above the right eye, with a protruding clavicle and possible broken left shoulder. Upon that transmission to the team at the hospital, a single flat line appeared on the heart monitor.

John had died. The ambulance raced through the traffic lights, which just changed to amber and heading for the hospital. The tall strapping young man, who chose a career as a Paramedic, began to sweat. Beads of anxiety began to run down the sides of his face and down his neck. He ripped open John's dressing gown and attached the paddles to his chest, hoping to shock John's heart to get a rhythm going. The Paramedic's continued life support and twice John's heart did not respond, and each time the Paramedic's had to turn up the voltage on the defibrillator. The third time John's heart began to beat softly inside his chest.

John had been dead for over Three minutes and unconscious from the early hours of last night till now almost six hours. The Paramedic didn't have a good feeling about this passenger. He had seen so many tragedies in his career, and certain situations gave you a gut feeling. This gut feeling was not promising. The Medic's pulled the stretcher out of the back of the ambulance and rushed John into the A & E department. All available trauma doctors had been called to attend. All available hands were helping in one way or another, ordering CAT scans, blood tests, x-rays. At this point John had lost at least two pints of blood. The doctors, at that moment, could not tell that inside John's brain was the worst possible scenario, that John's life was hanging in the balance.

Chapter 4

◆◆● ◆◆

The phone rang in John's Mum and Dad's house. They lived in a 3-bedroom Bungalow, just ten minutes outside of town. John's father was outside in the garden pruning the Roses every variation of coloured rose you could imagine. He loved spending time out there in the garden, it was his peaceful place. He loved to pick roses for his wife every morning and have them waiting for her when she walked into the kitchen. This morning John's mother was up earlier than her husband and was pottering around in the kitchen, clearing the breakfast dishes from the breakfast bar. She walked to the phone hanging on the kitchen wall when it gave its diminutive ring and she answered with a small "hello". Her hands clasped together as she cradled the telephone between her shoulder and ear.

The small "hello" was the only word John's mother uttered.

Gina had called John's mother to let her know that he had fallen down the stairs" during the night and that he was on his way to the hospital by ambulance, without another word, Gina hung up. John's mother dropped the phone. It banged against the floor then laid face down. She stood silently in the kitchen, her thoughts swirling and whirling around in her head. She always worried about John, even though he was grown with his own family. It's what a mother does best, worry. 'What had happened to her son?' she thought. Her husband of 50 years came in from the garden. He stopped in his footsteps when he saw the look in his wife's terrified face and the telephone on the floor. He dropped the bundle of red roses on the work top he had gathered for her and ran over to his wife just in time to catch her from collapsing onto the kitchen floor. He carried her over and sat her in a chair at the table and got her a glass of water. John's parents treasured each other. They had enjoyed every minute of their marriage and family life together.

John's father was born to working class but dignified parents who already had 7 children, when he came along. With another mouth to feed, when there already wasn't enough to go around, wasn't the kind of worry John's Grandfather needed. He was already overworked and terribly underpaid, but he did his best to provide for his family. John's father's given name was Leonard Blackmoore, but even as a wee lad, John's Grandfather saw the brute strength in his newborn son's eyes, a determination that would one day take him to greatness, a tower of strength for his parents and later in life when he met and married the love of his life, Joyce. Today would be the day that Len's true strength would be the only thing to get Joyce through what she was about to learn. When Joyce began to speak, it was in a very soft voice. Len had to ask her to repeat herself many times as her words were illegible at times. "We need to get to the hospital, John's been hurt!" Joyce finally blurted out.

Len left Joyce sitting in the chair and ran to the cupboard in the hall under the stair's and grabbed their coats and Joyce's Handbag and ran back to help Joyce stand up. He walked her out the door and into the car on the way to the hospital she reiterated the short conversation she'd had with her daughter in law. "Is Gina going to be there at the hospital?" asked Len "No" said Joyce softly, with tears emerging from the corners of her eyes and down her cheek's. "She said she had to go drop the kids off at school then to the office, they had a deadline" Joyce said tearfully. "What is wrong with her?" Len asked despairingly. "Her husband is in the hospital, and she has to go to work? What in the world is wrong with her?? I've never understood that girl". Joyce nodded her head in agreement. She wiped tears from her cheeks with a tissue she got from her handbag.

The drive to the hospital seemed like it took forever. It wasn't far away, but the anticipation they felt and not knowing what they would find when they arrived, made it tedious, they couldn't get there fast enough. As they pulled into the hospital car park, they found a spot as close to the main doors as possible, bought a ticket from the machine placed it on the inside of the window above the steering wheel. They sat in the car for a few minutes, each gathering their strength to go inside. They sat still and listened to the raindrops hitting the roof of the car. They didn't know what to expect when they walked into the Hospital.

Joyce knew in her heart that it was more serious than just a simple fall as Gina had described, a mother pick's up on thing's, she just knew it was more serious. In those few moments sitting in the car, Joyce began to reminisce about her son, and how he had grown up, so strong and caring. She remembered all the thoughtful things he had done, the memories that she had of raising her first son. She placed her soft yet frail hand on top of her husbands' strong and firm hand, their eyes met, and they knew it was time to go inside. He got out and went around the car and opened Joyce's door for her and gently took her hand and helped her out of the car, Len had a brolly he placed over the car door for his wife to take hold. As he closed the door his arm went around his wife's shoulder to comfort her taking hold of the brolly again, keeping Joyce dry. He was scared too but tried to hold on to his emotions.

They finally got to the doors of the hospital's A & E. Rain had really started coming down once they were inside. There was so much commotion going on inside the A & E department. Injured people lay on stretchers in the hallways; nurses trudged back and forth from cubicle to cubicle, carrying patient's charts. There were children sitting on their parents laps not able to sit still, crying begging for attention. The waiting room was packed, and it was only 8.30 am.

Len and Joyce stood there with all the commotion around

them, wondering who they needed to speak to. Nurses and Doctors were rushing about everywhere, in the hallways, were patients on Stretchers parked on the sides in the corridor as there was nowhere else, they could go. Len walked slowly with Joyce up to the reception area, nurses were sat down on the phone or filling out forms.

They waited for someone to notice them. A heavy-set nurse in a navy-blue Trouser uniform finally came over from behind the reception desk and asked what she could help them with. Len told her they were looking for their son, John Blackmoore, who had been brought in by ambulance this morning. Joyce stood hushed, almost statue like watching all the people in the adjoining cubicles. She heard her husband ask for their son. She turned her eyes towards the nurse in navy blue; Joyce noticed a name tag on her lapel that read Sister Margaret Evans. Joyce saw the look of condolence on her face when their eyes met. Joyce knew this was going to be a day she would never forget.

The Sister came from around the reception desk and said, "If you would like to follow me, we'll get you seated until the doctor can come and speak with you." Sister Evans gestured with her arm in the direction of the corridor and led them to a small almost bare room with a sign on the door that read "Waiting Room". Inside the room there was a harsh glow coming from an old table lamp that sat on an equally old end table. There were three chairs set side by side with another end table that was littered with old magazines. The pictures on the walls displayed landscapes in water colours from a local artist.

Sister Evans waited for them to be seated and asked them to wait there until she could track down their son's doctor. Sister gave Joyce a compassionate glance once again and turned and left them sitting.

Across the room, Joyce noticed there were more chairs like the one's they were sitting on, and another end table with a flower arrangement of what looked like Carnations. Joyce put her hands together and squeezed them together in worry, Len stared at the floor in silence. Len reached out his hand and gently rubbed the back of his wife's hand to reassure her. They could still hear all the commotion coming from down the hall in the A & E Department and reception. "Should we call Tina and Mark now? asked Len, Joyce nodded her head in agreement and gave Len her phone, he got up and stood out in the hall trying to get a signal. Joyce sat silently with her thoughts as her husband informed their other children that their brother was in the hospital

Chapter 5

◆◆●◆◆

Tina was busy getting ready for work. She had been up for a few hours already seeing her husband off to work and preparing lunches for her two boys and her daughter. Her two boys, Jamie, aged 9 and Christian aged 6 were running down the stairs towards the kitchen when the telephone rang. Her husband Paul had left for work an hour before. He was probably just arriving to open the shop and preparing for a busy day picking up the post by the front door. Christine with one of the boys' backpacks in hand, haphazardly stuffing books into it, ran for the phone in the sitting room as it rang 'Who would be calling this early in the Morning?' she thought. On the other end of the line, she heard breathing. "Hello?" T said the voice more forcefully for the second time. Her father's strained voice told her to come to the hospital, that John had had an accident. T's spine tingled,

"What happened? What is going on?" T asked her father anxiously. He could hear the panic start to rise in her voice. "All we know right now is that John was brought in by ambulance this morning and we haven't had a chance to talk to his doctor yet" Len paused and then whispered "your mother needs you T."

There was a lingering pause as both took a breath. "Dad, I have to drop the kid's off at school in five minutes and then I'll be there. Tell mom not to worry, I'll be there as soon as I can." With that, Tina hung up the phone and hurried back to her boys who were waiting by the front door with their coats on, ready to go. Jimmy the oldest saw the look of worry in his mother's eyes and gave her a reassuring wink and whispered to her as he leaned in for a hug, "Don't worry mum, everything will be okay." T knelt and leaned in closer and hugged her son tighter. He was so caring. She did the same to Christopher and then Alison running down the stairs into her arm's. Jimmy was distracted with the thoughts of the day, seeing his friends, and getting to play at school. She kissed both boys and Alison on the tops of their heads and hurried them out the door and into the car. She needed to call Paul her husband who worked in a printer's shop in town to let him know what was going on.

Amanda answered on the second ring. "Q printers this is Amanda speaking, can I help you?", Christine gave her a curtly 'hello' and asked to speak with her husband Paul. Amanda recognized Christine's voice immediately and her intuition told her that she was concerned about something. She gave Paul a shout and passed the phone to him.

Paul was working at his desk prioritizing jobs for the day on his PC, when he answered the telephone. "Hi Love." Without a pause between words T blurted, "John's had an accident and I need to go down to the hospital and be with mum and dad, can you pick the boy's and Alison up from school "? T could barely breathe. Her hands gripped the phone tighter and tighter. "OK, love, take a deep breath and tell me what you know." said Paul calmly "I don't know anything yet, Dad just called and said John has had an accident and they haven't spoken to the doctors yet." T switched the telephone from one ear to the other. Paul took a moment and then said " Listen love, you need to be there with your mum and dad, so go to the hospital, don't worry about the boys and Alison, I will explain here and leave early to pick the kids up from school. T sighed, told her husband that she loved him and that she would be home when she could.

As she drove to the hospital to be at her brothers' side, she remembered all the time when her brother John would make her mad, then make her laugh, then somehow managed to make her mad again. John always had this charm about him, like her father, you could never stay mad at him for long. There were times she'd catch John in her room when they were growing up, and she would find him reading her diary. No matter where she would hide it, he would find it. She would chase him out of her room, he would fly down over the stairs and she remembered hearing him giggle until his sides were about to burst.

She remembered when John at the age of five or six before Mark was born, would bring her a bunch of Daffodil's from the garden, when he knew something was on her mind. He had an innate sense of compassion. He would go out into the garden and pick a small bouquet of 'flowers' for her and come running back to the house with the biggest grin on his face, looking for her. When he found her somewhere in the house, his eyes lit up and brought out the 'flowers' from behind his back and yelled "Surprise". He would then jump up and down vigorously with excitement. He never wanted her to feel hurt. He was very protective over her. He would say in his boyish way that he 'would hit anyone who made her cry, as his little fists came up swinging wildly in the air. Christine remembered hugging him tight, and just when she thought she could never be mad at him; he would grab a small strand of her hair and pull. He would then jump up and run through the house, down the stairs and out the door. All the while, giggling and hearing Christine call his name throughout the house.

John's younger brother Mark was still in bed, Quilt wrapped around his legs and chest, only baring his arms. His head was buried beneath the comfortable memory foam pillow. He was dreaming of watching his brother John play in a local pub with the band from the night before. Mark had driven out to the pub where his brother was playing last night. John had never played better Mark thought. he dreamt about watching his brother up on-stage revel in the night's excitement. Singing and playing guitar, like never. The pub was packed with people. Everyone enjoying a drink and listening to the band play. They had already played the first set and were finishing the second set with Chuck Berry "Johnny B Goode" a big finish. The crowd were roaring "more, more, more" Johnny looked over at the Manager at the end of the bar, holding one finger in thee air, he nodded. He turned his head over his shoulder and said to the lads while setting the drum machine to the right beat "Status Que" "Rocking all over the world" Slight pause ...."1 2 3".

Mark had brought Sue his girlfriend to the pub to see his brother play. They had met a few months earlier when Sue was out with the girls in town, they had hit it off immediately. After the show, Mark dropped Sue off at her parent's house, walked her to the door and kissed her goodnight.

In that quiet place between dream and being totally awake, Mark thought he heard the ring of his phone on the bedside cabinet. The constant ringing brought him around to the morning light.

As Len dialed his son Marks number the phone chimed inside Mark's' flat. Mark lived 20 minutes away from the rest of the family. The answering machine picked up his dad's anxious words. "Mark, its dad. Come to Musgrove Park Hospital as soon as you get this message" Len closed his eyes, took a deep breath and continued, "John's been hurt, your mother and I are here now, and T is on her way." The answering machine caught the sound of Len hanging up the phone. The sound of the beep ended the message and the indicator light flashed on the tiny black answering machine that sat on top a wooden end table in the sitting room.

Mark flung the quilt back on the bed with one arm and sat on the edge of the bed trying to come to his senses and make sure he had heard the message on the machine from his dad correctly. John was hurt?? But? How?? When?? Mark couldn't imagine what had happened; he had just seen his brother last night, when he left the pub dropped Sue off then drove home. His alarm clock read a quarter to nine.

Mark stretched and yawned as he walked unsteadily towards the sitting room and clicked the listen button on the answering machine. The ancient appliance sluggishly rewound the tape inside of it and played Dad's message again. Mark listened to it at least three time's before he could move. Snapping back to reality, he dashed towards his bedroom and threw on his clothes from last night before, haphazardly buttoning his shirt as he grabbed his wallet and keys by his bed. He rushed to the front door pulling it shut with force, as Mark raced towards his car. He jumped in turned the ignition put it in gear and was off, Mark accelerated rapidly down the motorway, and headed towards the Hospital.

Chapter 6

◆●◆

Joyce sat with her mind picturing John as a little boy, such a cutie she thought in the brightly lit family waiting room, clenching a mound of tissue in one hand, and wiping tears with the other. Down the hall from the A & E department at Musgrove Park Hospital, Len telephoned T and Mark to ask them to hurry to their brother's side. As Len hung up the receiver, he glanced down the hall and noticed a tall man in a white doctor's coat turn the corner and enter the family waiting room. 'Maybe that is John's doctor" he thought to himself as he hurried towards the little room. Inside he found Joyce staring at the doctor, sitting as still as if she was paralysed by the fear of what may be. Dr. Shore stood up and shook Len's hand and introduced himself as John's primary Trauma Surgeon. Dr. Shore was a handsome man, in his early 50's. He had dark olive skin, with matching hazel eyes. A sincere looking man with a gold wedding band sat snugly on the doctor's left hand, and a green-checked bandana covered what hair he had left. Dr. Shore asked Len to be seated and then began to explain to them both, what exactly lay ahead for their son. Len held tightly to Joyce's hand as the Doctor looked up at them and said, "John has been assessed by our team and is right now, getting an MRI Scan, can either of you tell me the circumstances of what happened early this morning?"

Joyce and Len looked at each other and shook their heads, Joyce explained as best she could through her tears that she had received a call from their daughter in law Gina, John's wife, early this morning and all Gina told them was that John had fallen down the stairs and that she had called an ambulance and that they should get to the hospital quickly. Dr. Shore looked at the couple with a rather puzzled look on his face. He didn't see anyone who could be John's wife that was present in the room now. 'Where is John's wife?' he thought to himself but didn't ask at that moment.

"Dr." Len paused "How is our son?" Len asked. Dr. Shore took a long, unwavering breath and said, "Mr. and Mrs. Blackmoore, your son's condition is very critical at this point your son is not breathing on his own, so we have put a tube down into his lungs and it's helping him breathe, As I said earlier, he is getting an MRI scan at this moment, which is a computer-generated image of John's central nervous system. John has suffered an intra cranial hemorrhage. He also has a broken left shoulder and a contusion above his right eye." Joyce collapsed in tears into her husbands' arms and sobbed quietly. Len fought back tears too, showing his immense strength and internal fortitude as the doctor finished his diagnosis. "The hemorrhage we believe was caused by an aneurysm, or a weakened area of brain artery wall that has ruptured, once the MRI is complete, we will know exactly where the aneurysm has occurred, and we will prep him for surgery."

Len's' mind raced a million miles a second. 'How could John have all this wrong with him? Gina only said he only took a 'fall', he thought to himself as he cradled Joyce in his arms. There was obviously more to the story that Gina hadn't or wouldn't tell them. Dr Shore stood up, told John's parents he would send a nurse to tell them when they could see him and then said "If there are any changes you will be informed". He left the waiting room to check on John's progress. Len never liked John's wife Gina from the word go, but said nothing to John, because he seemed happy. As Len held his tearful wife in his arms he thought why, how, had Gina not known or said how serious John's situation really was? Len could not comprehend what had transpired this morning at his son's home. Len's thoughts turned to his beautiful grandsons Jason and Bradley. Did they know what had happened to their father? What had Gina told them? What had they seen?

What Len didn't know was that Gina had gotten Jason and Bradley to school without a word of what happened to their father. She had purposely kept them out of the sitting room where John's blood was still soaking into the carpet and what was a cozy family sofa. Gina kissed each of her son's and they waved goodbye from the playground. 'I'm not telling them what happened until I know where things stand' she said to herself. She also knew that she would have to call someone to clean up the mess before the boys got home, there was already too much to do today. Gina went back inside the house to the kitchen and on the laptop to find a local company who could clean up the mess. She found a small local company and dialed their number. The cleaning van was due to arrive later this morning and Gina had given them specific instructions as to what to clean and left the spare key to the house with a neighbour. She gathered her briefcase and keys and left for work.

As Gina drove down the motorway, she unassumingly hit the first speed dial on her mobile which was Lee's number. "Hello, love" answered a sultry and sexy voice on the other end. "How did you know it was me?" Gina giggled. The wind whipped in through the open window of the car, catching her hair and cascading it over the back of her neck. "I always know when your calling" Lee said, "Are we still meeting for dinner tonight?" Gina followed the curves on the road, lost in swirling romantic thoughts of the upcoming dinner with her lover. "Yes, of course we are, I wouldn't miss it for the world" she said getting a glowing feeling inside her tummy. They confirmed that they would meet at six pm. Lee insisted that he should pick her up. Gina politely declined stating that she would be at the office until late and would just run home and freshen up. She had never told Lee what her life really consisted of, meaning a husband and two children. She was an expert at keeping both of her lives very separate.

Gina said goodbye to her lover and hit 'end' on her mobile. As she continued her commute, she thought about just how much of a nuisance John was to her now and had been for quite some time. He did nothing for her anymore. There was no love between them, they had led such separate lives for so long now, but according to everyone in the 'outside' world and most importantly to the boys, they were still a happy family. Jason and Bradley didn't need a broken family. She didn't want her kids to become "statistics". Gina did her best to conceal her feelings of animosity and bitterness for the man she had been married to for 7 years'.

Her thoughts turned to when their relationship was wonderful. It seemed so long ago. A lifetime ago, she hadn't thought about those times in a very long time. She remembered that they had met in a nightclub where John's band was playing. Gina thought John was good looking. She envisioned him standing up on the stage, under the lights, looking like an impetuous carbon copy of Eric Clapton, his blonde untamed hair, being tossed wildly from side to side as his fingers made his guitar sing. Gina was standing at the bar with a drink in her hand while she gave him demure and coy glances throughout the night. Her hair was long blonde lightly curled flowing down her back, and she wore a white blouse and a black mini skirt.

Her ample and generous bosom fit snugly beneath the material. From under the shortest black skirt, John saw these long, elegant, and sumptuous legs. Gina took every man's breath away that night.

She watched John sing and play the guitar she flirted with her eyes, and he flirted right back with a wink of the eye.

All those many years ago both John and Gina felt like it was only the two of them in the bar that night. The atmosphere in the bar was lively with background music with a good beat. The music, the lights, the alcohol, was a dreamy cocktail. When the band took a break, John came right over to where she was standing and bought her a drink. He asked her name as he took her hand in his and delicately kissed the back of it. They never parted sides from that moment on. They were married within 12 months of meeting and Jason was born exactly nine months after the wedding. Gina recalled how happy life was then.

The car in front of Gina had quickly slammed on their brakes and forced Gina to come out of her dreamy state of remembering how life used to be. She pulled into the car park where she worked, parked her car in the closest spot she could find to the doors and went up to her office. No one spoke to Gina on her way to her office. She didn't speak to anyone either. She liked it that way. People kept their distance until they needed to get a final answer or confirmation on something.

A Van pulled up outside the house at 11.15am written on the sides was Busy Bee's Cleaning Company. They had strict instructions from Gina, they were told that the lady of the house would be out when they arrived, and they could find the

Key with a neighbour. Jenny was a slender Jamaican lady in her early 50's, was dressed in her

Work "uniform" that consisted of a pair of navy-blue shorts and a grey golf style shirt with the Company's logo on the left shoulder. She wandered up to the front door slowly and placed the key in the lock, she got from the neighbour and turned it, the door opened. She pulled a hair net from the pocket of her shorts and tucked her hair inside it as she made her way back to the van to get her box of trick's, cleaner for this cleaner for that. Pete, who had worked for Busy Bee's Cleaner's for 3 years was unloading the supplies from the van, when Jenny came back, she helped Pete pull the Electric steam-cleaner from the rear of the van. Jenny was a woman of few words but Pete on the other hand, liked to talk. Jenny said what needed to be said and didn't bother with small talk. 'If you're so busy talking, she would say, then you're not working'. Pete knew this but never thought any more about it. He pushed the steam cleaner up to the house following Jenny who was carrying a container of cleaning supplies.

'This job shouldn't take too long' Pete thought to himself, maybe he could finish early. It had already been a long morning for both of them. Jenny put the container of cleaning products down when she stepped inside turned to help Pete carry the steam cleaner through the front door. Jenny knew this wasn't going to be pleasant, and that this wasn't going to be a quick job. Her boss had told them that on this job, they would be cleaning up after an 'accident'. Jenny and Pete had cleaned some disturbing sites, but Jenny was used to it, Pete on the other hand didn't have the stomach for anything unsightly like vomit and things like that. Jenny's last job was as a cleaner in a Hospital, so she was used to seeing blood, and other bodily fluids and having to clean it but when Pete turned the corner into the sitting room, he immediately turned on his heels, put his hands over his mouth, pushed past Jenny and headed back out the front door. His stomach heaved and his head felt woozy as he leaned into the bushes beside the house. Jenny chuckled to herself "That boy" she said under her breath as she started to whistle a tune and shook her head from side to side. Pete gathered his senses and returned to the sitting room where he watched as Jenny lifted one of the cushions on the sofa, which was covered in dry blood. Blood soiled the arm of the sofa, and you could see where it had dripped down onto the carpet. "What do you think happened here?" Pete asked Jenny. Jenny shrugged her shoulders and mumbled in her sweet Jamaican accent "Look like a domestic to me now stop talking, were not here to make judgment or solve a crime, where here to clean up the mess, too many questions." Jenny just waved her arm in the air almost dismissing Pete. Pete still a bit queasy uttered "Well, let's get on with it, the sooner the better far as I'm concerned"? Jenny knew what Pete was like, once he got into the job he worked hard. From her experience at the hospital, she knew that by the amount of   blood that was left on the carpet, whatever had happened, had happened hours earlier. Jenny may not have been well educated in many things, but what she did have was life experience, and lots of it. They did their work thoroughly and dropped the key back to the neighbour.

Chapter 7

◆◆●◆◆

L en and Joyce were still at the Hospital in the waiting
room hoping to see John, when a Nurse burst in the
room and said "Are you John Blackmore's parents"
"Yes" said Len loudly.
"I'm sorry to say" said the Nurse. Len and Joyce thinking the
worst. "Your son has been transferred by Ambulance to
Frenchay Hospital in Bristol. "He has a bleed on the brain that
must be operated on as soon as possible". Bristol's the best place
for him the Ambulance won't take long to get there, she paused
thoughtfully rubbing her lip with her finger. "I know your
properly saying I don't know what I'm talking about, but my
father suffered a stroke 4 years ago which left him with
paralysis down his left side and short-term memory. My Dad's
a happy go lucky character always laughing about something. I

think that's what helped him recover, Mum still Say's he's a handful and a pain in the bum but we love him dearly".

"I'm sorry to hear that " Said Len sensitively, Joyce plucked up the courage and said softly to her""Well is John going to be alright". The Nurse with a gentle and compassionate look in her eye's softly said "Rest assured we are doing everything possible for your son" "Ok thank you very much" said Len sincerely, while hugging Joyce tightly with one arm.

The nurse turned and left the room. And then out of the blue the doors burst open. Len and Joyce jumped as if they had just seen a ghost. "Where's John how is he what's going on" said Mark and Tina simultaneously looking helpless yet showing concerned looks on there faces. Tina ran over to hug mum then Dad, Mark raised a hand and said "Hi" not one to hug or show affection. Len told them both what was happening to John "They've transferred him to Frenchay in Bristol he's got a bleed on the brain they must operate as soon as they get there. "Is that it" Mark said loudly "Christ is there nothing else we can do" Exclaimed Mark. Tina was quiet, deep in thought thinking of all the good times John and she had together when they were growing up before Mark was born. The holidays in the caravan at Croyde Bay. Making sandcastles before the tide would wash it away. The day's seemed to go so fast she thought and now my brother is critical in hospital about to have life saving surgery. And I was up set today when I broke a nail, catching it on my blouse. It seemed so pointless and insignificant in comparison to my brother's life or death situation, everything hanging on the edge. She hoped and prayed the op would be a success, one wrong move from the surgeon and that could be it for my brother. A little tier fell from her eye's her bottom lip trembled of the thought of it. Joyce could see her daughter and rushed over and gave her a big hug "John's a tough cookie T he's going to be OK love don't you worry. Len and Joyce always called Tina T ever since she was a little girl, She called John "Johnny B" when he was good and well behaved. Mark was Mark there were no two ways about it?

At that moment Mark chirped up and said "its times like this that you put thing's into perspective' 'Len nodded looking at his son, Joyce was still consoling T handing her a clean tissue from her handbag.

Chapter 8

◆◆ ● ◆◆

Gina's desk was cluttered with articles she was researching. Papers, books, and files covered the telephone as it rang sharply. Gina took the pencil she was editing with and shoved it in her hair that she put in a ponytail earlier.

She moved some paperwork and lifted the receiver. "Editing Department, this is Gina speaking, how can I help you? She paused for a second" Hello?" she repeated. After a few moments of awkward silence, she heard "John has got a bleed on the brain and has to be taken by Ambulance to Bristol for immediate surgery," She recognized the voice as John's father Len. Sitting up straight in her chair, she cleared her throat and said nothing. "What happened this morning, Gina?" said Len with an uneven tone in his voice "We need to know." Gina could feel the abruptness in Len's voice. Gina stated her opinion clearly "I don't know what happened, I found him in the sitting room on the sofa, and I called an ambulance". Len could feel his anger building like a volcano inside of him and he was ready to erupt. How dare she be so flippant about his son; her own husband may be dying? Blood rushed into his neck and cheeks. He had to contain his emotions. He was using Joyce's mobile he didn't want to seem upset while other patients and their families pass by in the corridor. He forced himself to speak calmly and rationally, "Gina, My son is having Brain Surgery! Do you understand what that means? "Len took a deep breath and continued with a sharp firm tone in his voice. "John may not make it Gina! Do you even care what happens to your husband?" Gina explained that there was nothing she or he could do for John, and that she had the two boys to think about. And that he shouldn't worry, John was in good hands". Len was ready to explode. Hearing her casual attitude made him furious. "Why are you being such an insensitive cow?" said Len, and added slightly louder, "What is wrong with you?"

He stood motionless in the corridor holding the phone firmly to his ear, tired exhausted his mind running at full speed in all different directions. Thinking if it were his wife Joyce, nothing else would matter he would be there by her side every step of the way.

Tina and Mark stood up and paced around the waiting room, each remembering the good times they had with their brother.

Len walked in from the corridor, handed the phone back to

Joyce. Joyce stood up "What did she say love" Len paused thoughtfully for a moment "She doesn't care" His tone changed to anger. " I don't believe that women how could she be so heartless" Joyce could see her husband getting in a state. She walked over to him and grabbed his arm "Come and sit-down love there's no point getting all wound up over that stupid woman, we need to concentrate on John' 'She paused. "We need to pray that he'll get through this. Her thoughts changed to Gina. We knew they had problem's she thought to herself, but we didn't realize how much.

"Right" said Len adamantly "Love let's go home get a few things and drive to Bristol". "I can't sit here doing nothing while John's being rushed to Bristol for surgery" Joyce agreed? T plucked up the courage and said "I'm coming with you I spoke to Paul earlier he said he'll pick the kids up from school" She pulled out her phone, out of her jeans to ring him again and let him know she was going. Mark gestured with his hands in the air I must get back to work. "Just let me know as soon as you know anything" Len and Joyce nodded. Mark placed his hand on his sister's shoulder to show some love and compassion. T understood showing a half heart-ed smile and kissed him on the cheek.

Chapter 9

◆◆●◆◆

L en drove cautiously, he hadn't driven to Bristol for a long time, It was about 45 minutes, they pulled into Frenchay Hospital. "Where do we park" T said. Len replied. " lets just head for the main building" They parked the car and quickly moved towards the electric double doors which opened when they got closer. Walking up to the reception. Len asked about his son, The middle-aged women with long brown wavy hair said " What's your son's name, "Oh John Blackmoore" Len replied She typed it in on the computer...."oh yes he's in Theatre now, if you go down that corridor and follow the blue line on the floor your come to a waiting area" she gestured with her finger, Your son will go to ICU once he's out of theatre." She pointed in the direction of the corridor.

They followed the blue line, there were 2 Nurses walking

towards them one holding some files and passed by. They continued to follow the blue line to a waiting area. Len, Joyce, and T took a seat and waited. It wasn't long before a young nurse in light blue uniform pushed open the double doors. "Oh, Hello can I help you". She said with an assertive voice. "We want to know how are son is doing"? Len spoke quietly. She said "Right Sir What's his name"? John Blackmoore Len replied anxiously.

"OK "She said She paused briefly "If you'd like to wait here, I'll make some inquires" She disappeared through the double doors. It seemed like a lifetime. The doors suddenly opened the Nurse said "He's in theatre now I'm sorry you'll have to wait". Len cleared his throat holding his fist to his mouth. I don't know how long he will be in theatre, if you'd like to take a seat. Len took a seat next to his wife, giving her hand a gentle squeeze.

They sat for 3 hours, T kept them all in coffee and biscuits from the vending machine and there was a loo close by. Suddenly the young nurse appeared again. "Mr. Blackmoore" she said, Joyce and T perked up. As she walked towards them, the young Nurse said. "Mr. Blackmoore your son is just out of theatre and there making him comfortable in ICU first, then you can see him, but you won't be able to stay long". They signed simultaneously as they sat thinking they'd have another long wait.

After half an hour or so the Nurse reappeared "If you'd like to follow me, I'll take you to your son" Len, Joyce and T got up and followed the young Nurse through the double door's passing the Nurses station and on through the ward.

A nurse rushing passed "Excuse me please" she disappeared into a side room. Another nurse appeared, Len looked at her badge, "Sister Wendy Smith" he mumbled to himself. They carried on following the young Nurse they got to a room the other end of the ward. Len, Joyce, and T were anxious not knowing what to expect.

The ICU Sister approached them "That'll be all Nurse" The young Nurse gestured with her hands and went about her business. Sister continued. "Your son will look different don't be alarmed they have put him in an induced coma to help with his recovery."

She opened the door lead them into the room as they followed her in Sister checked the monitors turned to them and said "I'm sorry but you can't stay long your sons just had major surgery I'll let you know when it's time. She left them closing the door behind her.

All three of them stood at the bottom of the bed looking at John, there were pipes and wires connected all over him, one feeding out to a respirator to help him breathe, monitors, a drip going into his arm, computers by his bed on both side's. They all looked daunted, gazing at all the lights dials and switches. They couldn't help hearing the respirator slowly moving up and down. T got hold of 2 chairs, she gestured with her other hand for Mum and Dad to sit.

T stood still at the end of the bed like a statue in disbelief "They've shaved all his hair off on one side" She thought to herself staring at the stitches disappearing around the back of his head. John would go mad if he could see himself, he loved his long curly blonde hair. They pulled the chair's closer to there son. Joyce held John's hand and rubbed it gently. She thought "Come on son you're a fighter you never give up, please god let him get through this" She was almost in tears.

Len put his hand on her shoulder, to comfort her.

At that moment Sister appeared. "I'm sorry" she said pausing for a moment to catch her breath "You'll have to go now."

As they were leaving Sister touched Joyce's arm. "Were doing all we can for your son, he's in the best place" she paused "We will look after him" lightly squeezing Joyce's arm Joyce half smiled. Sister led them through the ward, she opened the door to the corridor at the other end and spoke. "follow the signs to the main Reception and Exit"

Len and Joyce said "Thank you Sister" gratefully, T followed on behind.

Len was sat home in the kitchen drinking a cup of tea, Joyce was upstairs having a lie down, The Morning had taken it tole on her. Len's thoughts were of Gina not having a care about John, the man that had supported her and the 2 boys for years. "Dam it I'm going to phone her I need answers" he said to himself.

The phone rang and rang he was about to give up when she answered. "Hello this is Gina Blackmoore can I help you" There was a pause. "Gina it's Len we've been to Bristol to see John he's out of theatre and in ICU in an induced coma on life support, we really can't say anything else now" He said calmly.

Gina stood up and leaned on her desk, placing her weight on her right arm, crumpling some papers with her hand and said to Len "Well that's good, I cant stop now I have a deadline, I have a busy day ahead of me and have a lot on my mind, Could you call me at home later if there's any more news Len, I really have to go now." and hung up the phone like the receiver was covered with the plague.

While Len stood staring at the phone in his hand in disbelief, Gina's thoughts turned to Lee, the man she had been secretly sleeping with for the last ten months. They were meeting for dinner tonight at their favourite restaurant, The Bistro in Taunton. Lee always tried to get the quiet and very romantic corner table, in the restaurant. She dreamed of being held in Lee's arms with his deep blue eyes and athletic build, He was a very good-looking guy. His strong hands would hold hers; his strong arms would wrap around her like a glove, making her feel safe and secure. Seeing his warm smile made her melt. Gina's thoughts then returned to the husband that she no longer loved and who she had found lying on her sofa with a broken shoulder and swelling and bruising on the side of his head this morning. She shook her head as if to scatter these thoughts so far away from her that she would never have to think about them anymore and plucked the pencil from her hair sat down and began working again.

Before she knew it, it was half past three and she needed to get her boys pick them up and drop them off at her parent's house, for the evening. Gina finished filing her work, picked up her handbag and walked out of the building to her car and drove off. She arrived at the school just as the boys were running out of class. Gina gathered them in her arms, kissed and hugged them both, and shuffled them into her car.

On the way to her parent's house, both Jason and Bradley, in their excited ways, talking over each other at times, explained what they had done that day. If only they knew what had happened this morning Gina thought. They would never know what happened Gina said to herself as she pulled up outside her parent's House.

Gina's parents were in the dark about her and John's relationship as much as anyone was. Gina only told people what they needed to know and nothing else. She hadn't told them what had happened this morning with John either, but she would have too now. She would have to tell them something. She would have to play the part of the "loving and doting wife", only because she needed a babysitter for the boys, so she could meet Lee for dinner. Gina ushered the boys into the house as her parents stood there with arms open waiting for hugs and kisses from Jason and Bradley. She put the boys' knapsacks down inside the front hallway and watched them greet their Grandparents. Gina's Stepdad told Jason and Bradley, he had a surprise for them in the other room and led them down the hall. Gina's mother walked straight to the kitchen and put the kettle on. Gina slumped into the chair at the same worn wooden table that had been in her parent's tiny kitchen for as long as she could remember and put her hands over her face and broke down in tiers.

"What's wrong love" Her mother said in a Panic "What is it? 'Is it the boys? what"? Her Stepdad Martin heard all the commotion and appeared in the doorway. The boys were busy playing in the sitting room making car engine sounds. "What is it... what's wrong?" He spoke. Gina's Mother Jackie turned once again to her daughter and looked into her eyes. "Tell me what happened, love." Through bursts of tears, she pulled herself together and Gina explained, while Martin shut the sitting room door, so the boys didn't hear, She had found John, unconscious lying on the sofa in the sitting room this morning. Gina explained that she had phoned for an ambulance and how she had kept the boys away from the sitting room. Her Mother asked Gina what she thought had happened to John. Gina carefully thought to herself. If she gave too much information, or the wrong information, she would have to play things differently. So, she took a couple of deep breaths and told her mother that she didn't know what had happened, and that's when she had phoned the hospital later that day to get any information on John's condition, she was told that he was rushed to Bristol by Ambulance and straight into Theatre, Gina put her hands back over her face with her elbows on the table to hide what her mother might see on her face. Gina poured out all that happened that day. "You should be at the hospital" her Mother said, Martin agreed putting a hand on Gina's shoulder and rubbing it.

Jackie tried to calm her daughter down, as any mother

would. "Is that why you brought the boys, you want us to have them over night, cause you want to go to the hospital?" Jackie asked Gina trying to hide her elation; her mother had given her the perfect reason to leave. Her face still hidden, Gina uttered a hushed "yes" and pretended to sob into her own hands. Gina did feel bad for lying to her parents, but some things had to be done, and she would rectify the situation when she could.

Gina stood up, pushed the wooden chair away with the back of her legs and found a tissue in her pocket to wipe her tears from her eyes. She picked up her bag from the arm of the chair, turned back towards her mother and said, "Tell the boys I had to run back to the office and that I'll pick them up tomorrow." Jackie said she would tell them, as she watched her daughter leave and shut the front door behind her.

The evening air was refreshing to Gina's face. It cooled her skin as she walked to her car. Once inside her car, she took a few deep breaths and smiled excitedly. Now she could have dinner with Lee and spend the night in his arm's. She never gave the boys another thought or John for that matter. She was focused on Lee and there plans for tonight.

Gina drove off towards the motorway. She arrived back at her house in less than 15 minutes. After putting her coat on one of the coat hooks on the wall by the front door, she walked down the hallway and stood and investigated the sitting room, she was glad to see that John's blood was no longer still on the carpet or sofa. She turned around and walked into kitchen and blankly stared at the walls while she leaned her hips against the kitchen countertop. She could feel the coolness of the marble seep through the fabric of her skirt. It sent a chill up her spine. 'What happened to my life?' she thought to herself. 'Where or why did everything go wrong? She pushed those thoughts quickly out of her mind and hurried upstairs to shower. She couldn't wait to see Lee disappointed she wasn't going to stay. She needed him to hold her and say everything was going to be alright, she loved him to hold her tight and kissing her lovingly, "That's what I need" she thought, in his arms she felt safe and secure.

Gina phoned her father-in-Law, Len to arrange to go with them to see John in Bristol in the morning. Len was surprised but pleased she had phoned. "She has a heart after all or was it a guilty conscience" He thought.

Chapter 10

◆◆●◆◆

Gina was thinking of Lee, as she jumped in the shower changed her clothes and put some perfume on, Lee had bought her last Christmas. He was tall and lean, you could tell from his physique that he kept himself in good, physical condition. After the meal Lee had plans for them both. Gina explained to Lee the day's events about her deadlines with the paper. She didn't mention anything about her husband, he thought she was single and said she had to go and would make it up to him. She was exhausted and had to be up early. He understood "Text me tomorrow let me know how thing's are" 'Okay' 'He said She gave him a hug then kissed him on the lips softly and meaningfully. Walking away she turned and waved her fingers at him making a sad face and then left.

She had arranged to go with John's parents to see how he

was. The next morning Len Joyce and T picked up Gina from John's house, she seemed to take age's but eventually she rushed out turning to shut the door, coat, and handbag under her arm. It wasn't long they parked and went inside the hospital. They stood by the Nurses station in ICU and waited. Sister Smith appeared. "Mr. & Mrs. Blackmoore good a" She paused for thought '' Dr Rammie would like to see you he's the Neurosurgeon that operated on your son" She pointed at the young Nurse standing by the door. If you like to follow the Nurse, she'll take you to his office' 'Len knocked and opened the door to be greeted by his secretary quite a formal middle-aged woman with glasses. "Doctor Rammie will see you now" She opened another door and let them through. Len shook his hand and said "Nice to meet you." The Doctor said "please take a seat' 'Len, Joyce, T and Gina followed and sat down.

The Doctor sat and went through John's notes "Hmm, now" he said out loud.

'Now your son had a broken shoulder we re-set, more importantly he suffered a Intra Cranial hematoma" He paused reading the notes. "Hmm, a Brain Hemorrhage. 'he said thoughtfully to himself.

He let out a sigh as he straightened his back and settled back into his chair. his left-hand gentle scratching his brow and removing the cap from his head, As he'd just come from Theatre. He held it intently in his hand. Clearing his throat once more, the Doctor. took a breath and said, "John's operation went well he's in an induced coma, life support to assist his breathing we will be monitoring him for the next 48 hours." Joyce spoke up" Is my son going to be alright" holding a tissue over her mouth. The Doctor said" Mrs. Blackmoore. "The next few days are critical, but he's responding well to treatment".

The Doctor was used to seeing the relief and tears well up in his patients' families' eyes but didn't want John's family to have any false hope. He knew John wasn't out of the woods yet. He looked at all their faces turned to Len and Joyce. Joyce held on tight to Len's hand, she sat motionless as he explained John's operation. "John had an intra cranial hemorrhage." T leaned over and grabbed another handful of tissues from the box on the Doctor's desk and wiped away her tears, Gina just sat there looking around the room, as if she were waiting for a bus.

As the Doctor explained "When John arrived by Ambulance, They took him straight to Theatre' 'an aneurysm occurred in one of John's vessels in his brain. I want to be absolutely clear that this is not something he did or could have prevented." Dr. Rammie stated what exactly had happened to John, "An abnormal bulge or blister arose from a weakened area of a brain artery wall, and an aneurysm is caused when the weakened area of the artery wall expands outward and the vessel ruptures." Len coughed and put his hand in front of his mouth. The Doctor continued "Because of the amount of bleeding and pressure on John's brain, I had to perform surgery immediately."

T plucked up the courage and said "Will John be the same as he was before, when he wake's up Doctor". The Doctor said

"One step at a time it's early day's yet, As I said before, John is responding well to treatment that's all I can say at this time' 'taking a deep breath he said. "If you'd like to see him now speak to the sister on the ward" He stood up and gestured with his hand towards the door.

Len stood up and shook his hand Joyce followed holding his hand, she said "Thank you Doctor for everything you've done for are son" She turned away towards the door wiping her nose with her tissue. Dr Rammie was a serious man but showed a little smile on his face in recognition.

They all sat around John's bed quietly the only thing they could hear is the respirator going up and down keeping John alive. T played her MP3 Player with a Bluetooth speaker of John's band he used to sale CDs on gig's, thinking he might respond, After awhile she said look "his fingers moved" She said excitedly. "Really" said Joyce "Yes" T replied. I saw them move; it was his left arm" T smiled as if she'd just won the lottery. They all watched carefully. Things soon settled down again, Joyce though she was wishful thinking, mine you I think we all were, she thought to herself. Gina sat there by the end of the bed looking at her phone. "I wonder what Lee's doing"? She thought to herself.

"We best make a move" said Len. Joyce agreed. T squeezed her brother's hand "you get better, and I'll buy you a pint in your local" She thought. Gina was waiting outside ready to go. It was obvious Gina had other things on her mind and her husband wasn't one of them.

Chapter 11

◆●◆

At the same time as Jason and Bradley sat and played with their new toys at their grandparent's house, Gina was back in her car, on her way to meet Lee for dinner and John's family tearfully watched his respirator slowly laboured up and down, breathing life into his lungs, as he lay there totally helpless.

Lee was a man of impeccable timing; he was never late for anything, and he prided himself on it. He was in his early forty's and in perfect physical health. He had met Gina at a newspaper awards ceremony almost twelve months previously. He thought of the initial time he saw her. She was standing at the bar in the reception hall waiting to get a refill of champagne. He watched her intently, who she sat with, and whom she spoke with, trying to find something or someone in common with both.

Lee Williams was head columnist for a large newspaper conglomerate in Bristol. His lifestyle was lavish but had a shy and very conservative personality. Never being married, Lee was free to do as he pleased. He entertained his friends and co workers at his home with dinner parties. Women would swoon over him, but Lee rarely dated anyone.

He reminisced as he sat patiently waiting for her at their regular table in a quiet corner at The Bistro Restaurant. He saw Gina walk in and just as he had that first night, he watched her intently as she walked towards their table. Every man's head turned to watch this gorgeous figure of a women walk by as she passed each table. He was excited to see every man's envy when Gina approached him.

She was wearing the most delicious red silk Dress. Her hair was swept back with small ringlets of curls flowing down each side of her face. It had been too long since he had seen her. He loved her with all his heart. Lee stood up as she approached the table, extending his arms, ready to welcome her.

The candlelight, the music, the way Gina looked, he thought this night was perfect, and it hadn't even begun. As Gina walked toward him all she could think of was what the night might bring, what delightful and luxurious feelings they could share. They kissed tenderly and enveloped each other in a long, warm, and melting embrace. Gina felt her knees weaken. Lee reached out his arm and pulled out her chair and helped her sit at the table. He took his place on the opposite side of the table and extended his hand to hers, she took his hand in hers, they entwined their fingers on the pure white tablecloth, and the candlelight shimmered in their eyes.

As they enjoyed dinner, they talked of only themselves. They gave each other compliments, held hands, and Gina drank champagne from a tall, fluted glass. Lee caught the eye of the waiter pointing his finger in the air and asked him for the bill. He had carefully planned the evening, before Gina's arrival, but said nothing of his plans to her. The evening was going to be one luxurious surprise after another for Gina. Lee loved to make Gina happy, and Gina loved that about Lee.

His unconditional love for her was exceptional. It's what she'd always dreamed of, and nothing was going to spoil it. If Lee only knew that Gina was married with two children, the situation may be a little different, but Gina kept her life a secret from him as much as she kept this torrid affair secret from her family and friends. Gina made sure when they went out together that it was out of town, in a smaller place. Gina didn't think Lee had to know about her 'other' life.

What Gina didn't know was that one of John's band mates, Andy and his wife, Wendy, were celebrating their tenth wedding anniversary together with a romantic dinner at the same restaurant on that very same night. Andy's eyes were drawn to the red dress he had noticed out of the corner of his eye. Andy's eyes never wandered, he had the most beautiful wife in the world and was very happily married to Wendy.

Something was familiar about this woman in red. Andy gazed at her intently. Trying to place where he knew her from.

Wendy followed her husbands' eyes as they followed the woman in red to a table at the back of the restaurant. Wendy gasped putting her hand in front of her mouth and whispered across the table "That's Gina, John's wife, isn't her dress beautiful?" Andy blinked his eyes a few times and tried to see her face more intently. Wendy was right, it was Gina.

They both expected her to be meeting her husband. Instead, they saw her embrace, a tall, handsome man, a little bit older than John. They each silently tried to reason why Gina would be meeting him until; they saw Gina and this other man, kiss each other not just a peck, a full on the lips kiss, as if they had done it many times before.

There was no need for any explanation or rationalization after that. They knew automatically that Gina was having an affair. Andy and Wendy sat dumb founded as they watched Gina and her mystery man get up and leave the restaurant; they watched them searchingly for clue to say this was not an affair. To no avail, they could not come up with another scenario for Gina's behaviour. They couldn't believe what they were seeing, John and Andy were very close friends and not once had John mentioned that he thought Gina might be having an affair. It's just something John would have mentioned, even on a suspicion. Therefore, John mustn't know about it. Andy told his wife then and there that in the morning he would tell John about what they had seen tonight. John was too good of a friend not to say anything. Andy was furious with Gina. How could she do this?

But what Andy was about to learn the next morning would

make him absolutely infuriated.

Lee manoeuvred his candy apple red Porsche 911 around the circular driveway of his Detached House, pulling up close to the front door, and shut the engine off.

He turned slightly in his seat to gaze into Gina's beautiful eyes and said, "It's been too long, my darling". He took her hand and caressed the back of it as he lifted it gently to his mouth and placed a tender kiss on each fingertip. Gina felt as if she were literally melting into the seat of the car. Lee got out of the car, walked around to her side, and opened the door for her. Gina placed her left foot onto the driveway, the slit on her dress opened further letting Lee peek at her irresistibly long sun-tanned legs. Gina reached up to take Lee's hand and he helped her step out of the car. Still holding her hand, he reached back with his other hand and shut the car door. Walking towards the front of the house Lee placed Gina's hand under his arm, so she could hold his bicep as they seemingly floated up the two steps to the front door. With one hand on the small of her back, he opened the solid oak door with the other, and guided Gina inside the foyer.

Lee had done well for himself in the newspaper business. He moved up the corporate ladder rather quickly. He started at a local paper as a freelance reporter earning just enough to live on. Now he worked for one of the largest Newspaper's in the area and was well respected.

Lee loved to treat Gina. He'd buy her jewellery, perfume, sexy underwear, whatever she wanted. Lee was strictly a one-woman man though and wanted his women with the same monogamous outlook as he, if only he knew what Gina was really like, married two children a husband barely alive in hospital. He hadn't dated many women in his life, but he knew they appreciated the finer things in life. Only the best would do for Gina.

Chapter 12

ndy and Wendy awoke early the next morning, it was Saturday, and both were still thinking about the night before and what they had witnessed. Andy still could not imagine that Gina was having an affair, but nothing else could explain her actions last night. Andy had enough it was just gone 10 am he couldn't take it anymore the anger he felt inside and decided to go to John's house to ask Gina some questions. He knew John wouldn't be home, as the boys have football every Saturday till 12pm. So, he was safe in going to the house to confront Gina. Gina was in the kitchen that morning remembering all the evenings events from the night before when the doorbell chimed. 'Who could that be?' she thought as she walked down the short hallway. As she opened the door, Andy said to her " Stepping inside, 'Wendy and I saw you with another guy last night in The Bistro Restaurant?" He looked at her with fire in his eye's he was furious. To think his best friend's wife was carrying on behind his back. "I have no idea what you're talking about Andy, would you kindly explain why you've barged into my home?" Thoughts swirled around Andy's head; he was so angry; he didn't know where to start. "I thought you could do the explaining Gina" he huffed. "How could you do this to John?" Andy slammed his fist down on the banister that led upstairs. Gina was taken back by Andy's behaviour and stepped backwards into the side table.

The flower arrangement jumped in its place from the force of the blow. "How could I do what, Andy? "Are you mad? What are you talking about?" Gina blurted out. She knew she had been caught. 'He must have been in the restaurant with his wife last night for sure' she thought to herself. 'It's just as well' she thought, she too, had had enough of this Life of living a lie.

Andy told Gina of how he and his wife had seen her last night in The Bistro. He described her red dress, how she wore her hair and what Lee looked like. 'There was no denying it now' she thought. Andy and Wendy knew she was having an affair. As Andy was describing the events of the previous night, Gina stood there seemingly unmoved. Andy noted an air of confidence about her. Gina stood there not moving a muscle and composed.

Does John know? What do you have to say for yourself?" Andy said with a raised voice.

"In answer to both of your questions, no and nothing." Gina

said assertively. "John does not know how I carry on my life, and I certainly do not have to explain myself to the likes of you." Gina started back towards the kitchen to gather her things; she was on her way out to get some shopping when Andy rang the bell.

Andy followed her, even as she turned out of the kitchen and headed back towards the front door. "Would you mind leaving now Andy? I have some business to attend to." Gina opened the door and motioned Andy outside.

Once on the front step Andy asked, "When will John be home?" He knew he wasn't going to get anywhere with Gina, and he had to be the one to break the news to his best friend that his wife was having an affair. "The last I knew, John was going to Frenchay Hospital, Bristol by ambulance yesterday morning, if you want to know anything else, you'll have to go there and find out for yourself." Gina said calmly as she closed the front door. Andy stood there on the stone pathway in amazement. "What?? Why? What happened? Does he know what you've been up to?" Andy couldn't grasp what he was hearing. He couldn't believe that a man's wife could stand there and be so blasé and carry on an affair behind her husband's back and now to not even care that he was in hospital. "I don't know any details, my boys are with my parents and don't know anything either, so I would greatly appreciate it if you kept this conversation between the two of us." Gina announced. She started down the path towards her car. Andy again followed closely behind. "Are you going to the hospital now, Gina?"

Gina opened her car door and said over her shoulder "No, I've got some shopping to do." With that she got in the car and sped off out of site, leaving Andy standing there with his mouth open in disbelief.

It took Andy a few minutes to clear his thoughts and process everything that had just happened

here. As he sat in his car, he thought about some of the good times he had with John and Steve on and off stage. He hoped his friend was okay, He decided to go to Bristol for himself, he phoned his wife Wendy and told her what he was doing "Do you want me to come with you' 'She said "No Hun you stay home, I'll phone you when I get there' 'He paused for thought

"Bye love' 'he headed off towards the motorway, turning North towards Bristol.

Andy swerved into the closest parking spot he could find to the A&E Entrance. The usual hustle and bustle of A&E greeted him as he walked up to the Reception Desk. After a few minutes, the receptionist turned to him and asked him how she could help him. After explaining that he wasn't hurt, he explained that he was looking for his friend. "Well, what's your friends name? I'll look on the system." After all the utter confusion he felt after talking with Gina this morning, Andy almost forgot John's name. The receptionist waited for a few seconds before she heard the man standing before her say. "John.... John... Blackmoore is his name" Andy stuttered.

There was no need for the receptionist to look up on the system; she already knew what was going on with this patient.

She remembered his family, very kind, caring and loving family. She took a deep breath and asked Andy if he was related to John. Andy told her he wasn't. Andy could see the look of concern on the receptionist' face. He knew that she knew something about John, but was bound by doctor/patient confidentiality, and could not tell him what exactly was going on. "All I can suggest is that you go down this corridor, pointing with her finger. Follow the blue line it will take you to ICU" She added "I'm sure your find his family around there, they've been here since early morning."

Andy thanked her and made his way towards the corridor to follow the blue line. It wasn't long before he got to what looked like small waiting area with chairs in rows. A young girl appeared in nurses uniform light blue jacket and trousers "Can I help you" she said with a cheery smile.

Andy spoke up and said "I've come to see my friend John Blackmoore the young women in A&E told me to come here, she also said that some of John's family are here. She cleared her throat and said "Take a seat, I'll see Sister." As she disappeared through double doors.

Len suddenly appeared Andy stood up. 'Andy" he said surprised

"How are you" He paused "who told you about John" he said looking a bit confused.

"Hi Len, Gina told me, I got here as soon as I could, I rang Steve and left a message on his answer phone what's happened" He exclaimed.

"John has suffered a Brain haemorrhage after falling down the stairs"? "What" said Andy. "How did that happen; John's the designated driver he doesn't drink I don't understand I spoke to Gina just before I came up here" He pauscd. I better not mention I saw her with another guy last night" He thought to himself, "She said he's had an accident and was here" he rubbed his forehead with his left hand.

"Can I see him" Andy said "Of course, follow me" Len gestured towards the double doors, Len turned his head over his shoulder "don't be alarmed when you see him, he's on a respirator to help with his breathing. My God this is serious thought Andy. He opened the door slowly and looked around the room, there in the corner was John's Brother Mark lying back in a chair resting his head against the wall with his left arm on his forehead. Beside him was T holding John's hand, 'This can't be good' He thought to himself, as he stood still looking at John. After taking a few deep breaths, He noticed John had his hair shaved off on one side and stitches from the top of his forehead disappearing around the back of his head. Andy made his way over grabbed a chair and sat at the bottom of John's bed. He made a small cough into his hand. He wanted to get Joyce's' attention but didn't want to disturb anyone else. Joyce was sat in a chair on the other side of the bed, he nodded slightly to acknowledge her she raised a small but short smile Len let out a small sigh as his hands came down to his chin, and then sat up straight in his chair. "Andy was looking at John lying there helpless. "What have the Doctors said"? He said swallowing a lump in his throat. How did you find out?" Len asked.

Not wanting to spill the beans quite yet, Andy just said That he had run into Gina, and she told him that John was in the hospital.

Chapter 13

"I'm surprised she even told you that much." said Len annoyed. "She doesn't seem to give a damn about John and what he's going through at the moment". Well, Andy knew that much, after seeing her last night at the restaurant and her rather flippant attitude this morning. Now that he thought about it more, she really can't be that concerned about John at all, she knew he was in hospital and yet, she still went out for dinner with that guy. Who ever he was, madder and more confused than ever? Andy sat down in the empty chair beside Len and whispered, "What have they said about John?" Len's mind was swimming; he didn't know where to start. "We got a phone call from Gina yesterday morning saying that John was brought in by ambulance, Selfish cow didn't even say what happened or how he was." Len seemed just as bewildered as Andy felt over the whole affair. "Joyce and I spoke with John's Neurosurgeon Dr. Rammie he said John had an Indra Cranial hematoma a brain Haemorrhage followed by a stroke, it was because of the aneurysm he had suffered a stroke, the doctors did brain surgery yesterday to repair it" Len completely broke down then, for the first time in his life. He had been so strong for his family through the last 24 hrs that he just reached his breaking point. Joyce rushed over seeing her husband and held him in her arm's, his head lay on her shoulder. Andy stepped away and stood there not knowing where to look or what to do. As Joyce consoled her husband. "But how could this have happened, and when? John seemed totally fine when he left the gig' Andy thought to himself, he must have thought out loud because Len answered him. "That's what we're all wondering?" Len said, sounding more exhausted than ever. "What exactly did Gina say to you Andy?" Without wanting to get into hot water, Andy explained that "Gina had just told him to come here and find out for myself. Hearing this, Len became furious. He stood there stamped his foot on the floor, still holding Joyce with one arm around her and said, "Do you know she's only been here once and that was short and sweet?" "She doesn't care at all..." Len wiped his face with a tissue he pulled out of his trouser pocket. "She doesn't give a dam about John my son deserves better; she doesn't even know how serious his condition is." Len put his face in his hand and shook his head in disbelief and inhaled deeply. Andy felt uncomfortable he'd never been around this sort of emotion before.

They sat with there son for a couple of hours, as if Len could read Andy's mind he stated, "The doctors have told us that we should play some of his favourite music, it may help him come out of the coma." Andy thought for a minute. "Hay that's a good idea". Joyce was sitting at John bedside. One of her hands, gently rubbing the back of his hand she was doing what was maternal and she stroked John's forehead. Andy could also see that she was whispering quietly into his ear. Andy noticed that she was just as surprised as Len was when he first saw him in the waiting room. "Thank you for coming Andy. How are you?" said Joyce as she leaned into hug him. "I'm fine Mrs. Blackmoore, is there anything I can do for you?" Andy asked. "Just pray" Joyce said as she hugged and patted his back "Just pray." She repeated quietly. Andy stood at his friends' bedside, still in disbelief. Seeing John lying there connected to tubes and wires was unreal, considering less than twenty four hours ago he was standing on the stage with John and playing his guitar and singing his heart out to hundreds of people. Len suddenly said to Andy "Thank you for coming that means a lot to us, with a caring tone in his voice. "but how did you find out about John?" As Andy explained the short version of how he had ran into Gina and she mentioned that John was in hospital and it was serious, Andy stopped for awhile then said his goodbyes, "I'll bring Wendy up tomorrow, this has been a shock for Wendy and I" Andy said standing up and moving towards the door. Len and Joyce understood, they sat waiting, still no movement, John just lay there the only thing's that were working were the machines around him keeping him alive.

Joyce turned her head towards the door she felt there was someone there, Joyce looked up from her son's bedside with tears gently gliding down her cheeks. She stood up and wiped her face with the tissues she had tucked up the sleeve of her sweater and walked toward the doorway.

T appeared in the doorway carrying a tray of paper cups full of tea. "I thought we could all use one," she said quietly. As she placed the tray on a small table tucked in the corner of the room. She handed her father a cup, then she leaned over and gave her mother a cup. T got hold of hers and sat down beside the bed sipping the hot tea. John's head had been bandaged in white gauze. His face looked like it was falling to one side, like it was drooping a bit. Len guessed that was from the paralysis. His left shoulder and arm in a cast. John was not under a sheet or blanket. He was wearing a surgical gown and his legs were dressed in what seemed to be large white socks that went from his foot up to mid thigh, and these socks seemed to inflate and deflate in a quiet rhythm. "What are those for?" Andy asked John's parents when he pointed to the large white socks. "Those are to help John's circulation; it helps keep his blood flowing because he can't get up and walk." Len illustrated with hand motions by scrunching his hands into fists and relaxing them. Andy made his mind up right there and then; He would keep quite about Gina and her torrid affair with that guy until John gets better. He'd do anything to see his friend get out of bed and walk out of there as if it were all a prank "That's not going happen' He thought.

Chapter 14

◆● ◆

Gina finished her shopping and drove to her parent's house, to pick up the boys. As she put the key in the door it opened, the boys were coming down the stairs to greet her. Not saying a word, they ran in unison and ran into Gina hugging her. Gina enveloped both boys into her arms and squeezed them tightly. "Were you good boys for Nan and Grandad?" she asked. Together the boys let out a satisfied "yes mum' 'and then ran into the kitchen to find their Grandad. Gina's Mother came out of the kitchen wiping her hands on her apron. "How did it go love?" she asked as she hugged her daughter. Jackie just assumed her daughter had spent the evening at the hospital. If only she new the truth about her daughter Gina, they walked back towards the kitchen. Sitting at the table, Gina explained as best as she could, John had brain surgery and the doctors didn't think he was going to make it. That was it, short and sweet, no other explanation after all it was exactly what she heard in the telephone conversation with John's father earlier, so it wasn't a lie per say, she just neglected to tell her mother that she really didn't go or phone the hospital to find this information out. Gina kept her emotions in check, not wanting the boys to see her upset and left the explanations at that. She promised her parents to keep them informed when she knew something. Gina gathered up the boys' things and shuffled them off towards the car, thanking her parents who were standing on the front step, waving goodbye to Jason and Bradley.

On the way back home, she was lost in thought as to how to explain to the boys where their father was. She finally decided to tell them that their father was out playing with the band up north and wouldn't be home for a few days. They would accept that explanation and that would give Gina a few more days to figure out the rest of the details. A week had passed, and John's family still could not get in touch with Gina. They had left several messages on the Answer phone tried Texting her Emailing her nothing no reply, it was as if she had disappeared vanished, trying the house and at her office, but Gina had not returned any of the calls Email's or Texts. This annoyed John's family, they started to understand how bad their relationship was, their son's wife had not shown her face to check his progress. Some of those questions were answered on Thursday evening when Gina stood in the doorway of John's room. John's father Len had to hold tight to the wooden arms of the chair his elbows were resting on to keep himself seated. He desperately wanted to get up and strangle the Cow that stood in the doorway. He was a thousand times more furious than he realized. Gina stood there grinning like a Cheshire cat as she looked about the room. "So, how is he then?" she said as coldly and as callously as anyone had ever heard. She strutted into the room and glanced down at her helpless husband lying there in the bed and uttered a few words to herself. "Right, so who's going to bring me up to speed about John?" she said in a casual and unassuming tone. Joyce took one step closer to her daughter in law and scowled; "You don't belong here" she shouted at Gina and followed it with a stinging slap to the left side of Gina's face. Joyce stood her ground in front of her son's bed. If Joyce had anything to do with it, Gina was going nowhere near her son anymore. "You don't care about John, if you did you would be here at every opportunity" Joyce was livid. Len stood up and held onto Joyce's arm at the elbow to prevent her slapping Gina again. T held on to her mother's other arm. Gina let out a little snigger of laughter. She was undaunted by Joyce's reaction to her. "Well, it can't be good if Joyce is in such a mood" Gina replied and flicked her hair back over her shoulder. "Just who do you think you are coming in here a week later and wanting to know all the details?" Len said harshly. Gina just smiled and stated, "I'm his wife and if you won't tell me what's going on, I'll go find his doctor, it's as simple as that". No sooner were those words out of Gina's mouth, John's doctor, Dr Rammie walked into the room. Feeling the tension in the room was not very inviting. Although he had not heard the conversation that had just taken place, the Doctor knew something was not right. "Why don't we all go to the family room, and we can all talk there." he suggested and turned and walked back towards the door of the room hoping that everyone would follow. They all moved quietly down the ward following the Doctor who led the way. Gina trailed behind everyone and felt uneasy around John's family. She hated hospitals but she wasn't going to let any of them know. The doctor held the door of the family room open, and everyone took a seat. Gina sat on her own. She'd left the boys with her parents so she could see John and find out how he is? when everyone took their seats and stared in disbelief at Gina. "What's she doing here?" Mark asked his father. Len and Joyce sat silently.

They all sat upright in their chairs. Gina, who felt nervous because of her surroundings, did not let it show. She sat with her legs crossed and hands folded neatly on her lap. John's parents glared at their daughter in law. The doctor cleared his throat and said, "Now, I am assuming that you are John's wife?" Gina nodded her head as she glanced at Len and Joyce. They had not taken their eyes off her for a split second. Len was seething with anger and Gina knew it. "Could you tell me what's happening with my husband?" Gina asked the doctor politely.

Len stood up, "Why the hell should he tell you anything, you haven't bothered with John for the past week you don't care about my son." Len letting his emotions spill out, "You haven't made any effort to see or check how he is all week, and you have the audacity to ask the Doctor how is he'.' 'Dr. Rammie waved his hand in the air and said "This is not the time or place, we must concentrate on John's need's right now" he said trying to bring the level of anxiety down in the room. Len got up and marched out of the waiting room only to turn around and come and sat back down beside his wife. "You're right Doc, I'm sorry my apologies" he explained

"John is going to need a lot of love and support from his family right now" the doctor said, "He's in a coma from his brain injury and it could last for awhile". Gina seemed to take all of this information in and then asked, "Is he going to be the same person as before? What will he be like physically and psychologically, will he be able to walk, talk, read, and write? What's he going to be like"?" The Doctor cleared his throat and told her that John may be in this state for quite some time. "Brain injuries often take the longest to heal." The Doctor put his hand upon Gina's hand and added in a soft voice "John's memories, his personality, behaviours, his intellectual skills and physical abilities will all be affected, that's why getting him into rehabilitation as soon as he comes round from the coma it is imperative." Gina sighed heavily. "How long will that take" looking at the Doctor?" "I mean for him to come out of the coma" the Doctor glanced at John's parents and back at Gina. "He could be in a coma for up to a month or more, then with rehabilitation, I can't make any promises, but you will probably need to help him for the rest of his life." It was hard for Dr Rammie to have to talk to the families of brain injured patients, but he tried to explain the situation with the utmost care and compassion. "Thank you, Doctor" Gina said as she rose out of her chair and shook his hand. The Doctor stood up and said goodbye to the family and followed Gina out of the room, leaving John's parents holding each other's hands silently. Gina's eyes were fixed on the ground as she walked towards the exit; she just wanted to get out of the hospital and its sights, sounds and smells. She bumped shoulders with someone in the hallway. "Oh, sorry" Gina muttered and kept her head down. Once outside in the fresh air of the car park, Gina took a deep breath and signed.

She was glad she was out of the hospital. Her high heels made a tapping sound every time her shoes hit the road, as she hurriedly and made her way to her car. Once inside the car, she put her seat belt on and started the engine and sat for a few minutes trying to digest all the information she had been given by the Doctor. Leaving the Car Park, Gina glanced in her rear-view mirror and saw John's father Len standing in the road where she had just been, with his fist waving about in the air and screaming in her direction. "I'll deal with you later" she muttered under her breath and sped off towards the motorway. She knew now she would have to explain to the boys what had happened to there father.

Chapter 15

◆◆ ● ◆◆

D r. Rammie and the team of nurses were in John's room
when Joyce walked in from the canteen. She was
shocked to see so many people working on her son at
once. Seeing Joyce come into the room, the doctor gave some
instructions to one of the nurses who walked toward her smiling
that smile you know isn't made of good news. Outside the room
the Doctor said, "the swelling, or oedema, in John's brain has
caused the internal pressure in his brain to rise." He explained
it to Joyce with the example of hitting your thumb with a
hammer and the fact that your thumb is going to swell. The
brain reacts the same way, but the only problem is the skull
severely restricts the space the brain must swell.

The Doctor told Joyce that they were taking John down to
theatre for surgery and they were going to try to release some

of the pressure that had built up in John skull. If the pressure rises, they would be able to increase the drug levels to try to minimize the swelling. This was all too much for Joyce. 'Where's my Husband? Where is Len?' was all, she kept thinking after the doctor had told her that John needed more surgery. She didn't hear anything else. While she stood there wondering where her husband was, the nurses wheeled John past her out of his room and straight down the ward out in the corridor to theatre. Over the next 3 weeks John progressed. The swelling had reduced considerably in his brain; There didn't seem to be any movement from his right side. T noticed his left hand moved slightly. The doctors were sure that he was out of danger, but he still had a long way to go.

Joyce noticed that there was no movement on John's right side, it was lifeless. Joyce ran to the nurse's station and told them what she was seeing. Two nurses came into John's room followed by Joyce. They both stood around the bed, one each side, Joyce stood at the bottom of the bed and leaned in towards John, biting her lip. Both Nurse's did reflex tests and took his blood pressure. Just then Dr. Rammie came in the room, He was on his rounds. The swelling had started to get worse in John's brain the Doctor noticed from the computer next to John. It didn't require surgery this time as the Doctor released something in the drip hanging next to John. Joyce stood back at the doorway and watched everyone working on her son. She was beside herself with worry. The Doctor moved over towards Joyce and explained to her that she should contact the rest of the family and have them get to the hospital immediately.

Within what seemed like minutes, John's Dad Len and his Sister T arrived from the canteen. Mark was stuck in traffic. About 15 minutes later Mark rushed in, Dr. Rammie found them in John's room and asked them all to step out into the hallway for a moment. Joyce had insisted the whole time that any negative talk must be done outside John's room, and not where he could hear it. As they all gathered around, The Doctor told them that John was struggling, He's weak and not much fight left in him. The Doctor said putting his hand on Joyce's arm as tears rolled down her face, T stepped around to her with tears in her eyes to comfort her.

The swelling had gotten so bad that John's brain was bleeding profusely and said there was nothing more they could do. "Yes, there is doctor, we can pray" Joyce said forcefully. "I'll get a hold of the Hospital chaplain for you and send him right up" said Dr. Rammie. He hated that he had to walk away leaving John's family crying in each other's arms. He could still hear faint sobbing as he left the ward. About 10 minutes had passed when an old grey-haired man appeared by the door dressed in black with a white collar, holding a Bible. arriving at John's room with speed. He introduced himself as the Chaplain to John's family and asked them what he could do for them. Len gave him a quick review of John's situation and what the Doctor had just told them. "I see" he said sympathetically standing pensively at John's bed side. John's family wanted to give John a prayer of hope. Mark, T, Len, and Joyce stood on the left side of John's bed all holding hands while the Chaplain stood at John's right side.

The Chaplain spoke softly and said a few words, Blessing John "And dear God save this man please show mercy upon his soul ". The Chaplain could feel the love of this family of each other, and above all, for their son their brother. Joyce held up a tissue to her mouth and sobbed quietly. Len's hand held on tight to hers.

Len's mind was racing. He still didn't understand all of this. It was happening so fast. 'Were they actually going to have to bury their eldest son?' he wondered. The Chaplain continued, "The Son the Father and the holy ghost Amen. The Chaplain dipped his finger in a small bowl of holy water, stretched his finger towards John's forehead and anointed him with a cross of holy water. The Chaplain concluded the blessing with "Our Father who art in heaven, Hallowed be thy name, thy kingdom come, thy will be done on earth, as it is in heaven. Give us this day our daily bread. And we forgive those who trespass against us. And lead us not into temptation but deliver us from evil. For thine is the kingdom, The power, and the glory, forever and ever. Amen." Each of John's family whispered this prayer along with the Chaplain.

Joyce wiped her eyes and T hugged her tightly. Len put his arm around Mark to comfort him. Mark was upset, so let him. The Chaplain came to the left side of the bed and hugged Joyce and then T tightly. In Joyce's ear he whispered "Remember your faith, there's always hope my dear. Do not let anyone take that away from you." Joyce nodded and went to sit down by John's side and held his hand while Len stood behind her, with his hands on her shoulders.

Mark and T walked the Chaplain through the ward out the doors and into the corridor. "If you need me at any time, see one of the Nurses, they'll page me, and I'll be here as soon as I can" The Chaplain said sincerely. Mark and T nodded and shook his hand and watched him walk away, Bible in hand.

Gina was clearing away the dinner plates and the boys were quietly playing upstairs. She was trying to figure out a way to tell the boys about their father. They hadn't seen him for weeks and they were starting to ask questions more frequently. Her story that there father was out playing with his band, was starting to wear a little thin with the boys'. She called the boys downstairs and sat them down. "We haven't done anything wrong Mum?" Jason said with a face of innocence. She put her hand on his head and ruffled his blonde hair and said "no, silly, I just wanted to talk to you guys, I have something important to tell you." Bradley looked at his brother clueless. Not really understanding. Their Mother sat in the chair opposite the boys on the sofa. She stared at the floor wondering how to start the conversation. "Well boys, I have something to tell you" She paused thinking is this a good time to tell them about their father, then thought they need to know, I can't keep putting it off. She thought to herself This is not going to be easy to explain about your father." She stated. The boys looked at each other, then back to their mother. "Your father is in hospital" she paused to see the boy's reaction. They both looked puzzled. Before she could start again, Jason said "Well when is he coming home? I have a 5 a side football match tomorrow after school and he promised weeks ago he would be there to watch" Gina's back stiffened. "Well, the doctors don't really know when he'll get better" she said. "What's wrong with him?" Bradley asked and started to well up with tears in his eyes. They loved their dad. They did everything together. Bradley would help his dad in the garden, tending all the flowers. He even knew some of the flowers names the only thing was, he had trouble pronouncing some of them. Jason did sports and his father would take him and watch him play. John never missed a match. Now life was going to be very different for them.

Gina told the boys that their father had something wrong with his brain and the doctors were working very hard to get him all better. And that he was in a very good hospital with very good doctors and Nurses that were doing everything they could to help him.

They both wanted to go see their father. They begged and pleaded with their mother to take them. Gina told the boys that the hospital was too far away from home, and that the hospital had rules that only people over 14 years' old were allowed to visit anyone. There were no such rule and the hospital that John was in, was only forty minutes away, Gina thought to herself, at this point she didn't think the boys needed to see their father, with him connected to computers, monitors, and a respirator to keep him alive, she thought it might be too much for them. She hugged both the boys and headed them upstairs, to have their bath and get ready for bed.

Chapter 16

◆●◆

The tables turned almost overnight John continued to get better, after the Chaplain blessed him at his bedside, He seemed to grab on to every bit of life and got stronger and stronger. After nearly four weeks in a coma Dr. Rammie set a date with the family for him and Sister Evans to turn off the life support machine. John's family stood at the bottom of the bed, T said "what if he doesn't start breathing' with concern in her voice. "We'll switch it back on' said Dr. Rammie. The Doctor and the ward Sister stood by the machine and without any further ado, they switched it off. Len Joyce Mark and T literally held their breath, just as they were starting to panic, John took his first breath. They all signed with relief thinking it felt like he took a lifetime to grasp his first breath. "He's breathing" Mark shouted " Yes" with relieve. Joyce and T had happy tiers rolling down Their cheeks. "Thank you Doctor, Sister god bless you both" said Len trying to contain himself, holding Joyce with one arm and T in the other. "We will keep an eye on John" said Dr. Rammie. They then disconnected the respirator and pushed it against the wall. When the family had left, Nurses stepped in and removed the Tracheotomy tube from the trachea, leaving a hole at the top of his chest and cleaned him up.

As the weeks went by, Dr. Rammie administered injections to bring John out of his coma. Len and Joyce were having a coffee in the Canteen, when Joyce's phone rang. It was T "What's wrong love" Joyce said nervously thinking the worst yet again. "It's John, his eyes are opening, and I saw his left arm moving "T said excitedly like a teenager passing her exams. They could hear Mark in the background saying. "It's true, I've seen it". Len and Joyce both got up left their coffees and a half-eaten sandwich and rushed to John's bedside.

Low and be hold John was starting to come round from the induced coma, it seemed like life was flowing back into his body. It's a miracle, what more could we ask for thought Joyce. Sister Evan's entered the room and said "He's a fighter your son, we expect to move him onto the ICU Ward in the next few days.

Joyce smiled at Len, he gave her a hug and kiss. "I think this is just the beginning, for John, He's got a long road ahead love" he said looking very thoughtful. John was moved out of the room and onto the ICU ward, The nurses were checking John's progress though out the days to follow.

Dr. Rammie explained to Len and Joyce, that the severity of John's injuries will start to become more apparent as time goes by. They were already seeing improvements although his right side didn't seem to move. " Hc is now breathing unaided which is a good sign". Said the Doctor It had been one month exactly since John was admitted to Frenchay Hospital. Dr. Rammie said to Len and Joyce "your son is improving, and we will be moving him to Musgrove Park Hospital very soon'"? Len and Joyce were pleased.

The Ambulance took John to Musgrove on the Monday morning. The Nurses settled him in Shepard Ward. Len and Joyce were the first there to see him. There was more colour in his cheeks thought Joyce. Mark and T went to visit John several times while he was there. John carried on improving and after 3 weeks, He was moved to an independent building within the Hospital grounds. Alfred Morris Rehabilitation Centre, where patients both men and women were placed to recover, Rehabilitate, and finally be discharged. John spent over 4 months there, in that time Nurse Sue Tilley gave him an exercise book with lined paper. She told him to write each day's events down......."you know "She said "What you had for lunch who visited you on that day......She paused. "It will help you with your Reading, writing and above all your memory".

Well thing's progressed, one morning, the Nurses helped John into a wheelchair and pushed him down the corridor and into the dining room. Which doubled as a TV room. The Nurses introduced John to everybody. John wasn't aware of people at that stage.

Joyce and Len were sitting in the cafeteria one afternoon and Lex brought up the subject of Gina again. "Well, where has she been? Where are the boys? What has she said to them?" he questioned aloud. Joyce rolled her eyes. She was sure the boys were fine and as for Gina, well, Joyce's job was made easier if Gina wasn't around to argue with, she stated to Len. T had tried calling her numerous times and left numerous messages, Mark had driven by the house, but no one was ever home.

"I want us to go by the house on Saturday morning, just the two of us" Len said to Joyce. "Well, you better call her and tell her we're coming. I don't want any surprises", Joyce said with a firm tone in her voice. Joyce gave Len her mobile and headed back to John's room. Len made the call to Gina's office, the telephone rang, she answered immediately. Len was taken off guard by the sound of her voice. "Gina, its Len" he said in a quiet tone. There was silence from the other end. "Are you there?" Len asked. Gina cleared her throat and said yes. "Gina, listen, I don't want this to get into a screaming match, but I wanted to tell you that Joyce and I are coming by the house on Saturday morning." Len didn't leave room for her to say no. He continued "It's been too long, and I think we need to sit down and talk."

Gina coughed putting a tissue to her mouth and said "Len, Saturday isn't good for me. The boys have football" and before she could finish her sentence, Len interrupted "Gina, we are coming over to sort things out and that is final we will sit down together and discuss the future with John.

We'll be there at 10am" The telephone went dead in Gina's ear. She looked at the receiver in her hand and was in complete shock. Gina sighed and placed the phone back in its charger. She picked up the phone again and dialled her parents' number.

"Hi mum, it's me." Gina said cheerfully. "Oh, hello love, how are you, how are the boys?" Gina's mother said. "Oh, they're fine, listen Mum, I was wondering if you and Martin could take the boys for the weekend for me, they have football practice Saturday morning." "Oh of course love, we'd be glad to help you, is it John?" Gina's mother asked thoughtfully. Gina jumped on the lead her mother gave her. "Yes, I have to take care of a few things and would rather not have the boys deal with it too." "OK, then why don't you drop the boys off Friday after work" "That would be great Mum, thanks, we'll talk soon bye" Gina said, placing the phone back on its charger. She picked up her mobile, and dialled Lee's number, she was going to make the most of this weekend without the boys.

Gina had planned that she would drive over to Lee's place with an overnight bag, stay the night, go out that Friday evening for a late dinner and drinks, the boys would be at their grandparents, and then would come the unfortunate and uncomfortable task of sitting around the kitchen table with Len and Joyce on Saturday morning discussing what's happening to John. She hoped their meeting wouldn't last too long she wanted it over and done with, she didn't like that sort of meeting, especially when it involved John and his parents.

After the boys had been dropped off at her parents' house on Friday afternoon, Gina raced home to get ready for dinner. A long soak in the bath made her feel revitalized, clean, and sensual, she smelt and touched the top of her arm. Which was soft and smelt of rose petals. She looked in the mirror and thought to herself. "Lee won't be able to keep his hands off me" She smiled with a glow in her eyes.

John's situation never entered her head anymore that evening. She had her mind set on having a good evening with Lee. A nice relaxing meal with her lover, a few glasses of wine then back to Lee's, her mind and her body raced with adrenaline, she couldn't wait for Lee to hold her tight. All she thought of was Lee, the boys, and her work nothing else mattered.

Gina was dressed in a short black pleaded skirt with a light blue blouse and shoes. She looked amazing and she knew it as she took one last glance at herself in the hallway mirror, putting her lip stick on before she left the house.

The Tudor Restaurant was dimly lit, and the mood was quiet with a faint and subtle sound of soft music. The restaurant consisted mainly of couples eating and chatting some holding hands drinking wine in the relaxing, candle lit atmosphere. T and Paul had not been out to dinner together for such a long time and they welcomed their alone time with each other. They promised not to talk about the children or her brother John. Paul held T's hand across the table and gazed into her warm hazel eyes. T soaked up all the love she was feeling, as they finished their meal, T looked across the room and noticed that John's best friend Andy and his wife Wendy were also having dinner together. She wondered if she should interrupt to say hello to them. Andy had visited John often and been such a strengthening support system for her and her family. She told Paul that she had noticed them, and he asked if she wanted to go and say hello. They both got up and walked over to their table.

Andy and Wendy opened their eyes wide and smiled at Tina and Paul as they approached their table. Andy rose from his chair and shook Paul's hand and then stepped forward to hug T, Wendy did the same and said their hellos. "It's so good to see you" Wendy said to T. "It's good to be out without the kids" Tina smiled and looked at Paul. "Would you care to join us?" asked Andy as he motioned to their table. Paul said no, they had finished their meal and that they just wanted to come and say hello. "Well, it's no trouble you can stay and have dessert with us" Wendy said. T looked at Paul and Paul knew that T didn't want to leave just yet. "For a few minutes then" Tina said, and they all sat down together. The waiters cleared off Tina's and Paul's table to prepare for the next customers and then took their order for dessert.

Just as dessert was being served, Wendy had glanced towards the entrance of the restaurant and saw Gina, pretending to not lose interest in the table's conversation but not wanting to attract attention to who she could see, Wendy politely coughed into her hand, looked at Andy and motioned with her eyes towards the door, hoping that Andy would take the hint and look there without letting on to T or Paul. Without a word, Andy took his cue from Wendy and glanced towards the door. There he saw Gina with the same man as he had seen her with before and they were now being seated at a table across the restaurant. He coughed into his hand nervously and said to them "Can you please excuse me; I have to go to the loo". With that Andy excused himself and walked away from their table, but not directly towards Gina.

Andy paused at the door to the kitchen to catch his trail of thought. What exactly was he going to say? His heart was beating furiously inside his chest. He knew he needed to say something to them. He didn't want T to find out about her brother's wife like this.

After a few moments Andy straightened his tie, took a deep breath, and walked towards Gina's table. Andy had to be quick and straight to the point, he didn't want to cause a scene. Andy quickly walked up to their table and grabbed a chair from the empty table next to Gina's and sat down beside Lee. Gina caught her breath at the audacity of Andy. 'Who did he think he was' she thought to herself

"I don't think we've been introduced" Andy said as he extended his hand towards Lee. "Hi, my name is Lee, I'm Gina's" Andy cut him off abruptly with "workmate?" while shaking his hand. Lee smiled and said "No" and looked at Gina for direction. Gina was ready to leave the restaurant. She didn't know where to look or for the first time, what to do. That wasn't a problem for Andy though he said, "I don't think we've met before, I'm Gina's husband's best friend" and folded his hands on the tabletop and glared at Lee.

Now it was Lee's turn to look uneasy. He glared at Gina, raised his left eyebrow in confusion and tweaked his head to the right. "How could that be' he thought to himself. Gina instantly got up and left the table and headed towards the door. Lee stood up and Andy touched his arm and said, "Let her go, I think you and I need to talk" Lee didn't know which way to turn at that point and sat back down.

"So, I take it you didn't know Gina was married?" Andy asked him. Adjusting his tie and clearing his throat Lee said "Ahh, well, she did mention that she had been married but her husband had died of a heart attack years ago." "Oh, how rich is that?" Andy muttered and rolled his eyes towards the ceiling. Lee was so confused. He was thinking about Gina and where she had gone and trying to process this new information. "I don't understand" Lee said to Andy.

Andy glanced back towards his table and could see that Wendy was trying to keep Tina and Paul entertained but he saw that time was running out. Andy gave Lee a quick overview. "Listen, mate, I feel sorry for you ever getting caught up with that woman" Andy whispered to Lee "In fact her husband is not dead yet, but he is in Hospital and has been for months with a brain injury. She has been to see him once and their sons have never seen him since the accident. She is a very selfish manipulative callous woman" Andy could see the shock in

Lee's face. He even felt a little sorry for him. "My advice to you is get out while you can" with that said, Andy rose from his chair and headed back towards his table. Lee just sat there for a few minutes, staring at the tablecloth, and contemplating what had just transpired. He then stood up, picked up his napkin from his lap through it onto the table and headed for the front door.

Lee stood outside the restaurant; he saw Gina walking towards him. "Where did you go?" he asked her. "she paused "I just went to my car, I was going to leave, but I couldn't without talking to you first" she explained to him. "Let's not stand here and talk about it, follow me to my house and we'll have a drink." Lee suggested. Gina couldn't believe her ears. She was dumb founded. Either Andy hadn't spilled the beans, or Lee was more of an understanding guy than she thought. She nodded her head and walked toward her car. On the way to Lee's house Gina wondered what exactly Andy had said to Lee. Either way, she was about to find out.

They pulled up into the driveway, one after the other. Lee took Gina's arm and led her towards the front door of the house. Gina walked with trepidation. Lee didn't look angry at all. Once inside, he took Gina's coat and placed it over the banister in the hall and walked towards the sitting room. Gina followed him quietly. He poured them both a brandy and brought it to her as she sat on the sofa. "Lee, I need to explain" Gina said in a soft tone. As he kneeled in front of her, he put his index finger up to her mouth and whispered "Shh" he then stood up, drank his brandy down in one gulp, took Gina's hand and pulled her to him. Gina's pulse was quickening. She was caught up in a moment of disbelief that Lee was being so warm towards her while swirling in a moment of pure passion.

Chapter 17

L en and Joyce had been sitting in their car outside of Gina and John's house for almost half hour that Saturday morning waiting for Gina to show up. "She knew we were coming" Joyce said "That's why she's not here, I told you not to call Len" "I don't care if I have to sit here all day, I am not going anywhere until I talk to her" Len said sternly and hit the steering wheel with his fist. Joyce sighed. Her shoulders slumped back into the seat. Len's mind turned with emotion. What on earth could Gina be thinking he wondered, certainly not of John.

Just then Gina came around the corner of the street and pulled into the driveway. Len jumped out of the car, ready for an argument, leaving Joyce to exit the car herself. To his surprise Gina was defenceless.

As she got out of her car, Len could tell she still had the same clothes on from the night before. They were wrinkled and her hair was unbrushed. "Now, before you jump down my throat Len, let's just get inside" Gina warned pointing a finger at him. She quickly walked up to the front door, her handbag off her shoulder and Len could see her stockings peeking out of the side as if she rushed to get home.

This caught Len off guard, and he turned around to see if Joyce had managed to get out of the car and had followed behind them towards the house. Gina unlocked the front door and walked in, leaving it wide open. She dropped her handbag and keys on the side table and walked towards the kitchen to put the kettle on. Her mouth was dry and parched, she felt like she could murder a cup of tea at that point. Len and Joyce came in the front door and closed it quietly behind them. They hung their coats on the banister and followed her into the kitchen where they found Gina leaned up against the countertop with her head in her hands. She inhaled deeply and asked Len and Joyce to sit down at the table.

The events of last night had left Gina with a mix of emotions. All she wanted to do was get through this interrogation with John's parents and go to bed.

"Would you like a cup of tea?" Gina asked them as she removed three mugs from the cupboard. This attitude she was showing was not what Len had expected. He had prepared himself for a battle. To him it seemed that all the fight was gone out of her. Her shoulders were slumped, her face looked empty no expression. Her demeanour didn't deter him though from what he intended to say.

Gina put their cups of tea on the table and placed the milk and sugar beside them and seemingly cut Len's sentence off and said, "Let's drink are tea first before we start, shall we?" Gina didn't just merely suggest it, she demanded it. Len and Joyce just sat there quietly while they watched Gina drink her tea and stare out the kitchen window, deep in thought. Len couldn't take it anymore he had to start the conversation. "What is going on with you? Why haven't you been to see John?" he asked Gina. Gina took a deep breath. "How is he?" she asked as she clenched hold of her mug of tea with both hands.

"I don't think you have a right to ask that!" Joyce replied stammering with rage Joyce slammed her cup on the table spilling drops of tea onto the white lace tablecloth. "I don't want to get into a screaming match with you" Gina blurted, "I just want to know what to tell the boys". "Is that so?" Len said standing up and pushing his chair back with his legs. "You want to know what to tell the boys, well you would know what to tell the boys if you had come to the hospital to see your husband!" his voice getting louder and louder with each syllable.

"You two just don't seem to get it do you?" Gina shouted back at them. This time she slammed her mug down on the countertop. "I don't really care how he is doing, but John is the boys' father and I want to know what to tell them, they're bound to ask. "Gina said really agitated. Len was taken back by her comment. Could she not care about John? "What do you mean, you don't care?" Len's temperature was rising. Joyce couldn't believe her ears that Gina had admitted to not caring about John. Her thoughts turned to her son lying in the hospital bed, alone and helpless. Had John known her feelings towards him before his accident?

"John and I have been playing happy families for a very long time" Gina said sharply. "For the boys' sake." she added. "For everyone's sake". "Why?" Len asked. "If there were problems between you, surely you could have worked them out." Gina refilled her cup of tea from the pot. She didn't have the energy to go through the whole life story of her marriage to John with them. "Let's just say we agreed to disagree on many points in our marriage but wanted the boys to have both parents in the home." Gina continued "Now, I'm done with the marriage. I want out" Joyce who has been so faithful in her marriage to Len couldn't understand how his son could go along with this kind of arrangement with her. he knew the boys were John's life, that he understood.

Len's mind was reeling. "You want out??" "You want out?" Lex screamed at her as he stood up yet again at the table. "How dare you?!" his fist hitting the tabletop hard enough to make their cups jump up. "My son is fighting for his life and all you can say is I'm done, and I want out?" "What kind of monster are you?" Len was seething.

"I'm not a monster" she seethed back at him "I've just have had enough and want out of this marriage. The boys are old enough to understand things now and it's time to move on…"

she paused, "For the sake of all of us, I think you better leave now" Gina said as she walked towards the front door. "We've said all there is to say"

Len looked at Joyce. She could see the anger in her husbands' eyes. Len walked towards the front door and snatched their coats from the banister. "YOU will have to live with the consequences of this" he seethed as he handed Joyce her coat. Tears were welling up in Joyce's eyes. "Those poor boys..." she muttered as she put her arms into her coat. Gina opened the front door and stood there with her hand on the door. "You can come by next week and pick up his belongings" she said to them. "You will break my son's heart when you tell him this, cause I'm not doing it for you, I'm not doing it" Len said "I won't do it" he repeated as he brushed passed her and out of the house. Gina slammed the door behind them, she stood there with her back against the closed door and took a few deep breaths. "It's over" she whispered to herself and walked up stairs to take a shower.

Chapter 18

◆◆●◆◆

Andy and Wendy had slept in that Saturday morning. The warm sunshine shone through their bedroom window and gently caressed Wendy's face, slowly bringing her around to the light of day. She felt so warm under the blankets, curled up with her sweetheart and feeling the pleasant warmth of the sun on her face. What a perfect start to the day. Her thoughts soon turned to the events of last night at the restaurant. She turned over in bed and faced the window, away from Andy. His arm still draped over her waist. She thanked the heavens that she had such a wonderful husband and an incredible relationship with him. She loved Andy so much and she knew that her husband adored her too.

As she lay in bed Wendy thought how lucky it was that Tina and Paul had not noticed Gina or her mystery man at the restaurant. It was going to be hard enough to learn the truth about her sister-in-law, but T did not need to find out by seeing it with her own eyes. When Andy had returned to the table at the restaurant he apologized to Paul and T for being detained so long but he had run into a client of his on the way back and that they had chatted for a few minutes to catch up on a few things. T and Paul didn't mind at all. They enjoyed keeping company with Wendy. Wendy remembered how they had lingered or more like she had stalled them in to having an extra cup of coffee after dessert.

Wendy had wanted Gina out of the car park before she could let T and Paul leave.

Andy turned onto his back and stretched his legs under the blankets and then snuggled in closer to his wife, breathing in deeply the sweet scent of her skin. Wendy turned her face slightly towards her husband and gave him a tender kiss that said good morning. "What a night, last night" Andy sighed.

"You're telling me" Wendy said frowning, even though it was a serious matter. They both laid flat on the bed and continued talking. Andy gently lifted his wife's head with his arm, and she gently laid her head on his chest. "I was sure T was going to see Gina, especially when she stormed out of the restaurant like that." Wendy said. Andy replied "You should have seen his face when I told him John was not dead as she had told him" Wendy sat up, held the sheet to her bosom and shook her head "What did you just say? She actually told him that John was dead?" Andy eased her shoulder downward back towards the bed and Wendy laid back down and he said, "Yes she told him that John wasn't just dead, but that he had died years ago" Wendy gave out a gasp in disgust "She's really not a nice person my whole opinion about Gina has changed." she flicked some of her hair back and rested her head back on Andy's chest.

Gina walked into the bathroom and started the shower. As the steam filled the bathroom, she found herself sitting on the toilet with her face in her hands. The sound of the falling water in the shower muted her crying. "My life is falling apart?' she thought to herself. Her mind was distracted and flustered at the predicament she had found herself in. She knew that it was too good to last, this thing she had with Lee, but she didn't see it ending the way it had this morning. Clearing her thoughts, she stood up, undressed, and pulled the shower curtain back and stepped in under the waterfall of warm water the heated downpour of water washed the night before away. It cascaded over her hair and down her back, but it could not take her troubles away.

Gina's mind reviewed last night's events while she showered. She felt so close to Lee all night and then this morning so removed and distant. She didn't say much nor did Lee. He led her to believe things were OK.

He had met her in the car park of the restaurant. She was just going back in to find him to explain herself. He put his hand around her shoulder and told her to follow him back to his house which wasn't far away. As she drove in silence, Gina was glad that Lee had wanted to go back to his house and talk instead of screaming in the car park. She decided to just go in his house long enough to explain herself and then leave. She had no intention of staying the night.

That was not Lee's plan. Lee walked her in and sat her down in the sitting room and after a drink of brandy; he led her upstairs to the bedroom. He didn't want to hear any explanation. Gina's mind remembered the night's passion in a dreamy state while the heavenly warm water enveloped her body.

Those sultry thoughts came to a screeching halt when she reminisced about how Lee had woken her up just a few short hours ago. Gina was feeling so enamoured and romantic in her sleepy state in Lee's bed a few short hours ago. She remembered stretching her long legs and curling her arms around the pillow she had been sleeping on. Gina stretched out her arm to feel for Lee, but he wasn't there. She let out a hushed moan and stretched again.

All of a sudden she felt something soft hit her legs forcefully through the blankets. She looked and saw that it was her clothes that Lee had wrapped up into a ball and thrown at her on the bed.

Her eyes darted towards the bedroom door to find Lee standing there. He was completely dressed. Gina looked at the clock on the side table, it was 9.30am! She was going to be late to see Len and Joyce. That thought scattered from her mind quickly when Lee roared at her "Get up and get out of here!!!". His arm raised and his finger pointed to the stairs.

Gina stared at him uncertain and not fully awake. They glared at each other for what seemed like a lifetime. She didn't move from the bed; he moved a little closer towards her. Gina broke the silence first "What's going on Lee?" He roared "You are what's going on, I want you to leave." Lee continued "You have made a complete idiot out of me, and my heart is cut to pieces, and you still want more. Go home to your family Gina, we are through! "Gina grasped at the blankets and pulled them to her bosom. "I thought we were ok, Lee, what happened?" Gina said innocently. Lee picked up her shoes and tossed them on the bed. "We are definitely not ok, and neither is your husband judging by what his friend said last night, get out of here and never come back!" he shouted at her as he left the room. She heard his hurried footsteps going down the stairs.

Gina sat in the bed dumbfounded. She grasped the quilt in her fists. Tears streamed down her cheeks, melting the mascara that was left on her long lashes from the night before. Her clothes lay in a rumpled heap at the foot of the bed and her shoes were scattered either side. She wiped a tear with her left hand as her right hand stretched for her clothing. She quickly got dressed; her shoes dangled precariously in her fingertips and went to find Lee downstairs. Her bare feet skimming across each step, trying not to make any noise whatsoever.

With his hands in his trouser pockets Lee stood in the library and looked out the large window when he felt the presence of someone standing in the doorway. He turned and saw Gina there. Her hair tussled and makeup streaked down her cheeks. Seeing her like that, in that instant, he knew he shouldn't, but he felt truly sorry for her. "Why are you still here?" he asked her in a strong but quiet tone. Gina swallowed the lump that was in her throat and tried to speak. "I…I wanted to see you before I left." She stammered.

Lee turned toward her and sighed "Just leave, I just want you to leave" His hands came out of his pockets and motioned towards the door and in a tone that sounded defeated he said slowly "You lied to me Gina, you cheated me out of the only relationship in my life that I actually thought was going somewhere, you made me feel like a fool" Lee uttered through his teeth. "You gave no thought as to what I was feeling, never mind your' family, now just leave me alone, I wish I had never met you!" A single tear caught a glint of sunshine from the window when it floated down Lee's cheek; Gina saw it when he turned to face her.

Gina stood in place in the doorway and didn't move a muscle. She wanted to go and hug Lee because he was feeling so bad and yet she knew that he would never let her anywhere near him again.

"But, what about last night, after we came back here? Everything we said, everything that happened, I thought…." Her voice trailed off and her eyes cast downward. "Nothing was really said last night if you remember correctly, I kept cutting you off. You cannot play me like a finely tuned fiddle any more Gina, last night was my turn" Lee seethed as he took a few steps towards her. He placed his hands on the back of the brown leather settee and leaned on it. "You see, for the first time in my life last night, I was selfish, I got what I wanted, just one more night and now I'm throwing it away, just as you did with my heart"

Gina started to speak; her eyes still cast down when she was jolted back to her senses by Lee's voice. "GET OUT!!" He shook his head and pointed to the door. She had never heard his voice that loud before. Without another word, Gina turned and walked toward the front door. Lee walked around to the front of the settee and collapsed into it. His left arm rested on the arm of the settee, his legs stretched out and his hand wiped his brow. He was truly devastated about what had just happened.

Gina drove home, crying uncontrollably, she jumped in the shower analysing the events of last night, tears streamed down her face, the water cleansing her skin, but not her heart. She knew she would have to face a lot of things now and life certainly was going to change for her, but she didn't plan on facing anything until she got a few more hours of sleep. With her robe wrapped around her tightly and a towel around her head, Gina walked towards her bedroom to catch a few more hours of sleep.

Chapter 19

◆◂ ● ▸◆

John's progress had been slow after the accident. Len, Joyce, T and Mark were gathered around John's bed saying to each other how John was improving before they left for the night. Three months had passed since his accident.

When they were about to leave, John was trying to speak, it made no sense, but he was trying to communicate. The excitement and disbelieve was contagious, "did you hear that" T said they all nodded and rallied around John's bed. "How are you feeling son" Len said excitedly. They all waited for a response; John flickered his eyes, but nothing came of it?

"Are sons on the mend love" Joyce said to Len "he's on the mend" wiping a tear from her eye. They all felt positive about the future for John. Joyce was taken back with emotion, tears of relief welled up in Len' eyes. T and Mark hugged each other. T rubbed John's right forearm with her hand and whispered, "Welcome back John" and placed a small kiss upon his forehead. Len and Mark flew out down the ward to the Nurses' station to let them know what was going on with John. Joyce continually placed small kisses on her son's forehead until Len and Mark returned a few minutes later. "The doctor is on his way" Mark said excitedly as he flew down the ward to John's bedside. Joyce looked up and smiled at her youngest son. "Isn't this wonderful? Isn't this wonderful?" she kept repeating to everyone. T entwined her arms and held onto her dad's strong arm as they stood at John's bed side. Mark stood there at the end of his brother's bed and shook his head in disbelief and repeated to himself 'I knew you could do it; I knew you could do it'

After a few moments, Dr. Shore and a Nurse came and stood each side of John's bed telling the family to give them a few minutes to look and do a few tests.

Twenty minutes later, Dr. Shore stood in front of John's family again not knowing what to tell them. This time he didn't know what to say because of disbelief, not because he was trying to shelter them in any way.

Dr Shore took out his pen from his white lab coat pocket and initialled some paperwork on John's chart and as he placed the chart back in the receptacle at the foot of the bed he spoke in soft tones to John's family. "I am overjoyed that John has decided to open his eyes. I really am, this means his progress is getting better"

Joyce exhaled deeply. It felt like she had been holding her

breath since John was brought into the hospital all those months ago.

Doctor asked John's family to walk with him down to the family waiting room. They followed him excitedly through the ward and down to the end of the hallway

As they all took a seat the doctor stated, "When coming out of a coma, a patient may make incomprehensible noises and or move one or both arms or legs in a random and repetitive motion." He continued "They may often try to pull any tubes out, have facial expressions, groan, cry or shout. They may also try to move and may resist people doing anything to them. We don't know why they do this; it may be a matter of discomfort or pain for them"

He assured them that John's progress was well on track to recovery, but they would still have to be patient in waiting to see exactly how his brain had been damaged as far as comprehension and speech went.

He told them that John was breathing normally showing strongly that he could breathe on his own. Upon hearing that news Mark jumped up from his chair and threw his fist in the air in victory and let out a loud "YES!"

Smiling, the family listened to the doctor explain that John was still coming round from the coma, unresponsive state which meant that he would or could make a response when his senses were stimulated. His breathing and heart rate would increase, and he again warned them that John may make facial expressions and may have lost movement and feeling on one side of his body

Upon returning to John's bedside, two nurses made John comfortable. Over the next few weeks John progressed well enough for his doctors to upgrade his status to a conscious but unresponsive state. That meant that John was able to see, hear, touch, taste and smell but was unable to respond.

Joyce prayed and stayed at John's bed side the entire time. She knew all his nurses by name and most of them felt like old friends. They would speak of the day when John was finally be able to go home. It gave Joyce hope.

John progressed every single day.

He was in physiotherapy every day working on his physical abilities. A nurse would come in and wheel him down to the therapy room strapped in his wheelchair and he would sit there for a few hours working on one thing or another. John tired easily and he still could not respond to commands with speech, but his left side of his body was healing. The nurses told Joyce that they thought he would be up and walking soon. His muscles were getting stronger, and he was making tremendous progress.

When the physiotherapist had told her about John's perseverance in physiotherapy, she kissed John on the forehead and headed down the ward to the public phone. "They think he'll be walking soon!" Joyce exclaimed into the phone. T was ecstatic at the news that her brother had been doing so well. "Mum, do you need anything? Can I bring you something from home?" T asked. "Oh no love, I have everything I need here and besides, your father is coming in a few hours and he's bringing me a few bits and bobs" Joyce chuckled. "Well love, I better get back to John; will you phone Mark and let him know the good news?" "Yes, mum I will, you take care, and we'll see you tomorrow. Give John a hug from us, won't you?" T asked. "Hmm" Joyce hummed into the phone "Goodbye love" "bye mum" and there was silence on the line as T hung up the receiver.

Exactly three months after his accident, John's doctors gave him the green light to convalesce at Alfred Morris Rehabilitation Centre. He had successfully reached a conscious and responsive state. John could now respond to simple commands. Speech was still quite hard for John; he could make guttural noises and clicks but syllables and phonics were still out of reach for him. He could nod his head for yes and no when he conversed with anyone.

It was quite handy that Alfred Morris Rehabilitation Centre was located on the Hospital grounds. About half an hour from Len and Joyce's home, it would provide John with 24-hour care in a supportive environment. They had physiotherapists, occupational therapists, dieticians, and a social worker that would be on site to help John and his family. Dr Shore restated to Joyce and Len that the goal of rehabilitation was to help John regain the most independent level of functionality possible. He told them that rehabilitation channels the body's natural healing abilities and the brain's relearning processes so he will recover at his own pace, not necessarily quickly but as efficiently as possible. Rehabilitation would also involve John learning new ways to compensate, for his disabilities both mentally and physically, that have been permanently changed due to his brain Haemorrhage.

Alfred Morris Centre have trained staff that would give John all the help he'll need to recuperate and become more independent.

As Len and Joyce drove to the centre and parked the car. Len sat and looked at Joyce with a caring, loving look on his face. They spoke to each other through their glances.

They both knew that although there was a long road ahead of recovery for John, this was the perfect place for John to get started on his new life.

Walking towards the large white modern building, they could smell the flowers that were planted in beds outside, it felt welcoming as they walked towards the electric doors. The building was surrounded with beautiful gardens of flowers and shrubberies. The colours of pink's yellows and reds, the flowers were combined magnificently with the warm and dazzling luminescent sunshine with a slight breeze in the air.

Once inside the main building, Len and Joyce stopped and took in their surroundings. The foyer was charming and welcoming. The sunlight cast rays of orange and gold light onto the brightly coloured walls from the windows. The beige coloured floor was clean and tidy. To the left of the door there were chairs in a row against the wall. It offset the black wrought iron coffee table that sat just in front of them. There was a small flower arrangement of white lilies that were on the table. and nestled next to them were small palm trees on either side. Small wall mounted lamps cast a gentle warmth into the room.

Andy Twos, the Director of Alfred Morris Rehabilitation Centre waited in the foyer for their arrival. Their appointment was at 10am. He watched them enter and then approached them as they took in their surroundings. "Mr. and Mrs. Blackmoore" he said as he extended his hand to them. Andy was a tall athletic type with a strong presence. He was dressed in a formal grey pin stripe suit. His hair was black and brushed over the back of his head.

He walked over to them and introduced himself and shook their hands, Len took note of how strong and committed his handshake was. To him, that was a sign of integrity. He asked them to follow him down the hall to his office and on the way, gave them a brief outline of the Centres history.

In the hallway there were beautiful paintings on the walls. Joyce stopped and commented on one. "This scene is beautiful" she whispered. Andy came back towards Joyce and stood by her side admiring the painting and said "This landscape was done by one of our patients, in fact all of the paintings we have here are done by them, it's part of their recovery. Some patients didn't have a creative bone in their bodies before their accident. It's their way of expressing themselves."

Joyce nodded at Len. He knew what she was thinking. 'If this place takes as much care of the patients as they do their paintings, we've come to the right place'

They followed Mr. Twose down the corridor and into his

office. It wasn't a large office quite the contrary, it was functional and comfortably furnished. Joyce and Len took a seat, while Mr Twose took his seat in the high back leather chair behind his desk. They discussed John's needs for over an hour, Physiotherapy, occupational therapy, regaining his speech, exercising his limbs, to gain strength in his right side to enable him to walk and possibly make use of his arm again.

Joyce asked Mr. Twose about speech therapy. He replied "The speech produced by a person who has had a traumatic brain injury may be slow, slurred, and difficult or impossible to understand if the areas of the brain that control the muscles of the speech mechanism are damaged. This type of speech problem is called dysarthria" He continued "Once John's physical condition has stabilized, a speech-language pathologist may evaluate his cognitive and communication skills, and a neuropsychologist may evaluate other cognitive and behavioural abilities." Joyce and Len nodded in agreement. Dr Shore had gone over these items with them back at the hospital when they were looking at what was next for John. Mr. Twose continued "Occupational therapists would also assess John's cognitive skills related to his ability to perform "activities like day to day living" such as dressing and preparing meals and an audiologist will be assessing his hearing."

Mr. Twose asked them if they had any other questions and Joyce asked if they could be shown around the Hospital. He told them that he would get someone to take them around He was just going to a meeting but Sue Tiley the sister would gladly take them around. Mr Twose picked up the phone on his desk, spoke and mentioned a tour around the hospital. "Thanks Sue" he said before hanging up. "Sue will be here shortly and she'll show you around."said Mr Twose as he got up out of his chair. She arrived a few minutes later, knocking on the door before entering. Len and Joyce stood up as Mr. Twose introduced them to Sue. And then followed them out the office, Mr Twose once again shook Len's and Joyce's hand before heading down the corridor.

Sue was a woman who looked to be in her early thirty's. She was dressed in Navy blue trouser uniform. Joyce noticed that there was no wedding ring on her left hand.

Sue showed them around the facilities. Len and Joyce took in as much as they could as they casually walked from room to room. There was a large conservatory that overlooked the enclosed garden. In the conservatory was a library of books against the far wall, loads of comfortable seating and placed at the other end was a wooden table with six wooden chairs two were carvers. Sue pointed out to Len and Joyce to look at the enclosed garden, landscaped with shrub beds and a pond in the middle. A path from the patio wound around the pond and garden like a snake, flowers in full bloom were so colourful and lush.

Sue suggested they take a seat in the dining room at one of the tables. They had been walking around for a while and she thought that it would be nice to sit and take a break and to also have a little chat with them about what they do here at Alfred

Morris.

Sue took a deep breath and asked Len and Joyce if they had any questions so far. Joyce commented on how beautiful and peaceful it seemed to be. Len commented on the well-kept garden and how tranquil it was. "patients and staff enjoy sitting out in the garden, it relaxes them, which is good for both patient and staff" Sue replied.

Sue stated "I've been a Nurse for over 10 years now and this by far, is the best rehabilitation Centre around. You can see it in the patients' eyes, they love it." "Mhmm, yes, I agree" Joyce said as she gazed out the window. Joyce turned and looked again. "Is that a peacock in the garden." All surprised. Sue replied. "Yes, that's resident peacock Percy" As she smiled at them both. "Well, I never." Said Len smiling from ear to ear. "Getting back to John's needs" Sue said getting Len and Joyce focused again. Len said to Sue "What are some of the therapies John will be doing here?" "Well," Sue said "The goal of any rehabilitation is to help the individual progress to the most independent level of functionality as possible. Each person's needs are different." Sue pointed out. "The physical and mental rehabilitation programs help the patient to progress at their own pace, in many ways, it comes down to what the patient and his or her team of workers have set out for themselves." Sue paused for a breath looking at both.

"It could be that the ability to express needs verbally in simple terms may be a goal. For others, the goal may be to express needs by gesturing with their hand pointing at things or people." Sue picked up her pen and toyed with it doodling on a piece of paper in front of her, the goal of therapy may be to improve the ability to define words or describe consequences of actions or events. "It depends on each patience's abilities and needs; John will be assessed when he arrives here. Sue looked at Len and Joyce and said, " Are you both happy with what I have just said" she cleared her throat. Len and Joyce nodded their heads. She continued "The cognitive and communication problems of traumatic brain injury are best treated early, often beginning while the individual is still back in the hospital. This early therapy will frequently centre on increasing skills of alertness and attention." Sue paused, took a breath, and watched Joyce and Len momentarily to see if she had 'lost them'. She added "Patients will focus on improving their orientation to person, place, time, and situation, and stimulating speech understanding." She continued "John's therapist will provide oral-motor exercises to him if it is determined that he has speech and swallowing problems." "I do hope I'm not going over your heads with all this information?" Sue added sympathetically. Joyce wrapped her hand around her other arm as if she were giving it comfort, "We've both been through so much in these last four months with John and have learned more than I thought my brain could handle at times". I understand Mrs Blackmoore, it's a lot to take in, but your son will be in good hands" Sue said confidently. Len added with a chuckle "Most times when you watch a medical show on television, you have no idea what they are talking about, but once you have been through what we have with John and in the hospital as often as we have, you tend to pick up a few things along the way"

"Is there any other questions about the Centre or its facilities that I can answer?" Sue asked John's parents. Joyce looked at her watch on her arm and then at Len "Ah," Len said, "That look means, we best be getting back to the hospital". All three of them laughed out loud. Sue escorted them back to the foyer and before they left, she said, "Sometimes when we leave, we have more questions that we didn't think of, so if anything comes up, don't hesitate to give us a call" She outstretched her hand and shook both of theirs. "It was a pleasure" Joyce smiled at her and turned to leave, taking hold of Len's hand, the automatic doors opened, and they walked outside. When they both sat in the car they turned and looked at each other, Joyce said "This is where John needs to be" Len agreed "Definitely" He replied. "They have trained Doctors and Nurses that can help John get better what a perfect place to bring John." Joyce exclaimed and looked at Len with hope in her eye's. Len reached over to Joyce and planted a kiss on her cheek, she looked back at him thinking, you saucy man, showing a little grin. They headed back to the main hospital to see their son.

Chapter 20

◆◆ ● ◆◆

T he Nurses had sat John up in his bed with a couple of extra pillows John nodded for "yes" when T asked him if he wanted to sit up in his bed a little higher. Joyce and Len entered seeing their son sat up, Joyce's eyes glowed with such happiness as she gazed upon her son's soft green eyes. She leaned him forward and added another pillow behind his back. She was truly content with his progress. She knew in her own little way of knowing that John would one day, be up and walking and talking again. Joyce noticed John wasn't happy with something she couldn't understand what he was trying to say. She called over a nurse who replied "I'll get Dr. Shore he'll look at John I won't belong" And scurried off down the ward. Dr. Shore appeared shortly after. "I just need to examine John' 'The Doctor was deep in thought. After a short while he appeared pulling the curtain back from around John's bed. "John's got double vision in his right eye, it's not unusual for this to happen, we'll put a patch over his eye for the time being which will alleviate any discomfort, It should rectify itself in due course.

Space was limited at Alfred Morris and John was lucky enough to get a bed rather quickly and in only a few hours it would be moving day for John. He was on his way to Alfred Morris Rehabilitation Centre. John had gone through a battery of tests in the last few weeks. It was determined that he suffered with short term memory, which meant he couldn't retain information that was just presented to him. This happened when he had his aneurysm. His long-term memory from before the accident had not been affected although he did not remember the hours before his accident. Dr. Shore had explained to John's family that short term memory simply meant that John retains information such as digits or a small number of items for a short period of time without creating the neural mechanisms to recall that specific information later and that long term memory occurs when you have created those neural pathways for storing ideas and information which can then pass and be recalled weeks, months, or even years later. John had a long road ahead of him and as his family watched, he gained strength more and more each day. John arrived at the centre around eleven in the morning. He was glad to feel the sunshine on his face and breathe in the warm air as he was wheeled into his new residence. Joyce and Len pulled into Alfred Morris Centre a few minutes after John had arrived. They were excited for this day and for John. It had been a long, tough, uphill battle, but John was making remarkable progress. John would become frustrated with his self, progress was slow, but he never gave up. You could see the determination in his eyes every single day.

The Nurse at the Main Desk gave Len and Joyce directions to John's new room. When they arrived, John was sitting in his wheelchair, looking out his window, his eye sweeping back and forth trying to take in all the beautiful landscaping outside. John had a private room with bright white walls. It made the room surgical but there were 2 pictures of Landscapes on one wall, making it a bit more homely. A large display of mixed flowers flowed out of a vase placed on a corner shelf where John could see them from his bed. Opposite John's bed was a TV hung on the wall, Len thought John's got everything here to encourage him to make progress. His son certainly was showing perseverance. Len was so proud of him.

Chapter 21

◆◆●◆◆

The following day, John was washed and dressed and put in a wheelchair and pushed into the dining room. After breakfast as it was a nice day John was wheeled out onto the patio with a few other patients, it was a lovely day with the sweet smell of flowers and tranquil surroundings left him feeling relaxed, content for a moment.

Len wasn't angry, more disappointed at this latest display of Gina's character, he wanted his son away from this woman. The sooner the better, as far as he was concerned the marriage had been over along time ago. He knew it wasn't going to be easy for John to understand that his wife had left him. He thought there isn't a right time, but he needs to know, how will he take it he thought, Talking about kicking a man when he's down. But Len would make sure that John had all the proper help necessary that he would need. Joyce shook Len's arm and whispered "love?" Len came back to reality, the memory of the conversation with Gina quickly dissipated in his mind. Len cleared his throat. "I must have wandered off for a few moments". Joyce smiled up at her husband, "We better go now if we want to see are son. Looking intently at his wife, Len muttered yes, hugged her, and left to get his jacket from under the stairs "Can you lock up love" Len called to her, "OK Hun" She replied.

It wasn't long before they parked the car outside Alfred Morris. They walked in and down the corridor to John's room. "Oh" said Len peering into John's room. "John's not here". Joyce called over one of the Nurses passing in the corridor. " Could you tell me where our son is please" The Nurse politely said "Some of the patients have been put outside on the patio. They walked out through the conservatory and out onto the patio and there was John. "Hello Son" Len said. Joyce gave him a hug and kissed him on the cheek. John tried to smile but something was stopping him. Joyce picked up that something was wrong. She looked at John he was trying to say something. "Gina's gone" he slurred with a tear in his eye just about to fall. Len and Joyce were taken back, they looked at each other. "He spoke" Len said really surprised. "He said something about Gina, I'm going find out what this is all about." said Len with a slightly confused look on his face. Marguerite John's social worker saw them from the conservatory and wondered over. "Mr. and Mrs. Blackmoore can I have a word, it's about yesterday" "Sure" Len said. "John had a visitor yesterday, his wife, she wanted to talk to John in private, so I let her use my office, She was only here a few minutes and then left". By the time I got there, John was in bits, I don't know what she said but she left John in a hell of a state?" "What a cow, she's showing her true colours now' 'said Len. "I'm sorry I get so annoyed when I hear her name, I won't involve you in are family disputes, but Gina his wife has a lot to answer for' 'said Len with an infuriated look on his face.

Joyce took hold of her husband's arm "Darling let's take John back to his room" Joyce tugged Len's jacket. "OK love let's get him inside.

The weeks turned to months after three months of speech therapy, physiotherapy, and occupational therapy every day. John was managing to walk short distances by locking his weak knee on his right side when placing his weight on it and using a stick to assist his balance. His speech was improving all the time, he could string a basic sentence together but often it was a yes or no. Joyce, Len, Mark, and T were regular visitors who could see the improvements John was making, and they were all so please to see how John was doing. He still had no feeling in both his right arm and leg, but his double vision in his right eye had gone.

After lunch a week later John had some visitors, He was sat in the dining room watching TV drinking a cup of tea. When in walked two guys. John thought I know you. It was his band mates Andy and Steve, John recognized them as they got closer.

"What do you want" John said slightly slurred. "You haven't lost your sense of humour then" said Steve laughing. John extended his left hand out to shake their hands. "Hay your looking good' 'said Andy "what's the food like here' 'said Steve. "It's... not... bad. it could be worse" replied John. They stayed for a couple hours, chatting, and laughing about all sorts, even some of the places they played at. Steve jumped in, 'do you remember that pub in Bristol in a back street it was more like a cider house, and this drunken guy had a broken leg in plaster, and he was dancing swinging his crutches around, when he knocked someone's pint over' 'They all laughed. "I thought oh no there's going to be a punch up, but the landlord came around and had a word with the bloke with crutches and he sat down the rest of the night, not a word, I reckon the landlord told him to sit down or he'd break the other leg." They all laughed in fact John hadn't laughed like that for a long time and then Steve looking at his watch said. "I've got to get back I took the day off and the wife's got some jobs she wants me to do around the house. "Nice to see you're on the mend John" Steve said "Hay I'll be out of here soon' 'said John looking quite determined. Andy said "I'll be in again John soon' 'with a smile on his face. "See you guy's oh Andy "John said as Andy turned his head over his shoulder. "Up ya Kilt." Your right said Andy turning to Steve he hasn't lost his sense of humour.

Chapter 22

◆◆●◆◆

Joyce was at Alfred Morris visiting John, Len dropped her off that Saturday morning so he could meet Mark and pick up John's belongings from his house, as agreed with Gina on the phone. Joyce wanted to take John into the dining room, John said "wait a minute' 'Joyce looked puzzled, he locked the wheels of his wheelchair as Joyce watched him slowly stand up. "Mum pass me my stick please" he said with some urgency in his tone as he was a bit uncertain on his feet. Joyce watched him slowly walk to the dining room with only the aid of a walking stick. She was over come with delight to see her son walking. "Don't over do it son" she said walking behind him with her arm's out just in case John lost his footing. "I'm ok Mum really, thanks" Which made John more determined. They sat and had a cup of Tea the radio was on low in the background, a staff member came over with some biscuits, "Thank you Helen" John said. She introduced herself "I'm John's Physiotherapist Helen you must be his mother. Joyce nodded. "Call me Joyce" she said. "I can not believe he's come this far in such a relatively short time" she said gratefully. "Thank you for looking after my son" Joyce said with appreciation in her voice. "That's alright" said Helen with a big grin on her face. "John's come along way and has the determination to achieve, which makes thing's easier, I only wish all the patients were like John, it would make my life so much easier." She said looking at John with admiration. " I have other patients to see and no doubt we will bump into each other again soon, it was nice to meet you Joyce" said Helen as she turned and walked away. Joyce half heartedly put her hand up with a slight wave. Helen turned and acknowledged and disappeared down the corridor. "Well son it's nearly lunch time, are you hungry." Joyce said smiling. The large serving hatch opened where they served the meals each day. Staff appeared pushing some patients in wheelchairs to tables and others managed on there own. When everybody was seated the food was served, John knew the menu off by heart after being there nearly four months, it must be Chicken with veg and new potatoes and gravy he thought, It's all in my diary he thought to himself. Low and be hold John was right as one of the staff put a plate in front of him. "That looks good son" Joyce said. One of the staff asked Joyce did she want another drink she nodded "Tea please with a sweetener .... thank you". Once lunch was over the Nurses helped some of the patients back to there beds as it was time to rest or sleep for an hour, this happened every day. Joyce knew the routine she looked at John and said "Your father will be here shortly to pick me up, were both be in tonight to see you Son. She placed a hand on his shoulder and lent down and kissed him on the cheek. "OK Mum see you later" said John as he got up from his chair and slowly made his way back to his bed.

Chapter 23

◆◆●◆◆

Early Monday morning Gina arrived by John's bedside demanding him to unfreeze the accounts. She said "I can't pay the mortgage" John remembered he did freeze the accounts which were in his name. I thought she would help herself and she had he thought. John said "Gina your have to pay it yourself" She replied. " I'm not using my money" looking at John as if he were an idiot? "Well, you're going to have to, I'm in no position to pay the mortgage' 'John replied assertively but with a slight slur. She stormed off in a huff. The next day Gina turned up with Bradley their youngest son who was 3years old. He was so pleased to see his dad. He gave him a big hug, John used his good arm and hugged him back thinking why as she suddenly brought Brad here, his eyes were welling up, he seemed different they grow so fast John thought. Gina wanted to go outside for a smoke, she pushed John outside in his wheelchair. Bradley sat on his dad's lap going out into the garden. They sat down near the pond, Bradley got off his dad and was running around and watching the fish in the pond. John told Brad to be careful, next thing Bradley was running around the little wall that surrounded the pond. Oh my god Brad fell in the water and went under. Gina shouted "Do something" jumping up from her seat. "I can't" John shouted in despair? She hurried over to the pond put one foot in and grabbed Brad. "We need a doctor" Gina shouted in desperation. She placed Bradley in soaking wet clothes on John's lap and said "Hold him there I'll get somebody"! And rushed off inside. A Doctor checked him over and said "You're a lucky young man Bradley' 'Facing John and Gina the Doctor said when Bradley fell in the water, the water was cold which made his body tense up, that's what saved this little man" He looked at Bradley and said " You won't do that again will you Bradley. Bradley shook his little head from side to side and then hid behind his mother clutching her leg.

T and her husband Paul arrived early evening at the Hospital, they found John lying on his bed listening to music through a MP3 Player. He got up and slowly sat on the side of the bed and said "Hi" T with excitement in his voice. Do you want to watch a film" T said John looked at her. "OK what's the film" John replied unsure. "Oh, you'll like it, its right up your street" T laughed. They all walked to the dining room, Paul set the DVD up in the machine, they all then sat back to watch.

Nearly two hours later the credits rolled up on screen, still laughing John said " That was brilliant, T and Paul agreed all laughing together. "Well, we have to make a move, were come down again soon John" Paul said still laughing at the film.

Up bright and early, John sat in the dining room having breakfast surrounded by other patients. Margarita his social worker sat down beside him and said " Would you like to go out for a drive and maybe stop for coffee somewhere" John looked at her, " Great, what for" He said curiously. "We need to see if you can cope with travelling in a car. "I know it seems silly, but with a head injury like yours we need to know if you can cope in a moving vehicle, is that alright John" John grabbed his bad arm from falling. " OK what time" he said excitedly. "I've spoken to your wife who agreed to go with us, so it will be you your wife Angela a nurse and myself". She slowly stood up "Did you understand that John" as she looked at him. "I do" John replied.

Gina arrived shortly after breakfast; joining John in the dining room was Margarita, John's social worker, walked in the room with Angela the nurse. Are you ready Margarita said to John and Gina, both nodded and stood up? John and Gina followed them to the car, Margarita suggested John sit in the front. Angela started the car, and they were away. "If you feel nauseous or any discomfort at any time John, just say" Margarita said. John turning his head and nodded. They drove out of town and up into the hill's where they stopped at a pub called The Traveller's Rest. It was an old pub with low ceilings,

John ducked his head to avoid the beams. They stopped for a coffee for 20 minutes and then got back in the car and returned to the hospital. Margarita and Angela congratulated John and they both said "we had our doubts at first but well-done John, you've done very well today " They both sounded content, happy and relieved all in one. John was just happy to get out of the hospital, but it did tire him, so he went for a lie down on his bed. Gina got in her car and went to collect the boys from her mother's. Len had other things to deal with today, He had to phone Gina to arrange a time to go and pick John's clothes and things up from the house. After three failed attempts, this was the day. Gina had made up another one of her lame excuses about why they couldn't come over. Len remembered the conversation, "Gina, we are coming over on Saturday and we will pick up John's things his guitars P.A and all his clothes. You want John out of your life for good?" Len yelled, "Then I will certainly help you, because no son of mine should ever have been caught up with a woman like you!" He remembered how Gina's temper just blew up on the telephone. She screamed through the line at him "Woman like me? You bitter and twisted old man, you want John's stuff? I'll make certain you have every piece that belongs to him" She slammed the phone down in his ear.

After a time, Gina calmed down, but she was still very angry that Len spoke to her like that. She sat on a stool in the kitchen sipping her cappuccino, she was in deep thought about the things Len had said. Maybe I should go back and visit John and tell him it's over, she thought to herself and having no thought for John's condition? That's it, I'll go now I'm in the right frame of mind. She dropped the boys off at a neighbour's, she got in the car and drove down the motorway, after 25 minutes she parked outside Alfred Morris Rehabilitation Centre. She sat there for a moment took a deep breath and got out of the car and walked towards the doors. In the foyer there were people passing by coming and going Gina stopped Marguerite as she was passing by. "Excuse me Marguerite can you tell me where John is please"? "John he's having lunch now Mrs. Blackmoore" She spoke with a very stern tone. "ooh" Gina replied. your husband is doing very well as you saw when we went out for a drive" said Marguerite. "Hi, remember me Mrs. Blackmoore I'm Sue Tiley the resident manager here at the centre." She extended her hand. Gina shook her hand and said "I've come to see my husband." "Well John's having lunch now would you care to wait here" Sue spoke firm but friendly. "I'd like to have a word with him, alone, somewhere private please" "Ok you can use my office it's just down here; I'll find John first" And she walked off to make inquiries. Gina waited, she was nervous, not at all comfortable in these surroundings with that clean sterile smell in the air. Sue returned "Mrs Blackmoore John was having lunch he's just finished now and, I've wheeled him into my office where you can speak to him in private" She beckoned Gina to follow her down the corridor. "He was tired after are little trip out today, so he's using his wheelchair Well this is my office, if you let me know when you've finished, I would be grateful I'll be in the foyer". "Thank you' 'Gina replied as if she was on a mission. She opened the door to find John in a wheelchair facing her, He didn't look like my husband any more she thought, she thought that when they were out for coffee, he seemed more like a stranger. She stood in front of John and said "John I have 2 cheques for you to sign one for £300.00 and the other for £200.00" Looking sincere as if she cared, John struggled but managed to sign them both and like Jackal and Hyde she changed. "Look your only half a man, I don't want you back, so you better find somewhere else to live, oh these cheques are for your clothes musical equipment and your Guitars " She turned and left closing the door behind her. John sat there trying to process what had just happened tears started to roll down John's face. Margarita saw Gina walk past and out to the car park she knew from experience that there was something wrong.

She got up and hurried herself to Sue's office where she found John tears streaming down his face. She stood by John putting a hand on his shoulder, John put his good arm around Margarita's waist and hugged her tightly, while tears rolled down his face.

Chapter 24

◆◆●◆◆

It was Saturday morning the day Gina agreed that Len could pick up John things. He drove over to Marks place, Mark had already rented and picked up the van. He was waiting in the van for his dad. Len pulled up he parked and got out the car, walked over to the van his head was down cast and got in the passenger side. Mark, without saying a word, put the van in gear and drove off. Both were silent throughout the entire journey to John's house. Both were lost in their own thoughts. As they pulled into John's Street, Mark's stomach dropped, he could see John's house from the corner where they had turned. Len's eyesight wasn't that great, so Mark knew his father could not see what he was seeing up the road. Mark said there's something wrong with the engine. "Just a minute I'll have a quick look under the bonnet" Mark said to his father as he pulled over to the side of the road. Mark got out, lifted the bonnet, and pretended to poke around at this and that. He had no idea how he was going to stall his father, he needed time to figure out an explanation. Suddenly Len was standing beside him at the front of the van. "What's the matter with it?" he put his hand on his youngest son shoulder. "Oh, who knows, this van is old dad, could be a number of things" "Let me have a look son" and pushed Mark aside. Mark rolled his eyes. Len said, "Start her up son" Mark knew he couldn't put the inevitable off much longer. He jumped into the seat of the van and turned the key part way. The engine wheezed and groaned at only being half started. "Try again" Len yelled from the front of the van. As Mark went to turn the key for a second time, he noticed that a car was pulling up alongside of the van. He thought maybe someone was coming to help them. Mark left the keys in the ignition and jumped out of the van to see who had pulled up. There to his disbelief was Gina, sitting in her car smiling at Len. "We're just on our way to pick up John's things" Len said to Gina trying to retain his anger and hate for the women. "Oh, I know you are, and I'm on my way out." She said as she leaned her arm out the window and rested it on the door. "You'll find everything in order; all of his belongings are there." Len shook his head as he leaned on the front of the van, "There.... where?" he asked a little bit confused and looked around. Mark knew what the answer was. The answer was the reason he pretended to stall the van and pulled over at the top of the street. "At the front of the house" Gina blurted out "I must go, I have to pick up the boys from Mum's" she said as she pulled away rather quickly. Her hand waved in the breeze.

Len stood there and watched her drive away. He shook his head, rubbed his eyes, and looked at Mark. Mark tried to avoid his father's glance. He felt so bad for him. He had to deal with so much and Mark knew all this commotion was ripping his father's heart apart. ""'Come on dad, let's get this over with" Mark sighed as he put his arm around Len's shoulder and led him back to the passenger side of the van and opened the door for him. As Len sat down, he looked at Mark and said, "You knew, didn't you?", never taking his eyes away from his fathers, Mark admitted to making out there was a problem with the engine but not because he knew what Gina was up to, but because he thought his father had been through enough lies and deceit from Gina without facing more.

As they pulled up and stopped in the driveway, Mark's eyes glanced over at his father. His Dad was Silent not a word, Len's eyes rolled up and down. Len shouted "How has it come to this? How?" He raised his left arm and pointed to the pile of what looked like rubbish on the front patio of his son's home. It was only when you looked closer into the pile that you could tell that the pile was made up of John's belongings. His clothes, guitars in their cases, speakers an amp's. All of John's belongings lay strewn in a heap on the patio outside the front door.

It was a while before Len and Mark could believe that Gina could do such a thing. "She must have got somebody to move it all for her" said Mark turning off the engine. After a while, Mark said, "Well dad, it's not going to move itself" and without saying a word, Len opened the van door and got out.

Gina hadn't put anything into boxes at all. It looked like she had literally opened the window above and threw everything onto the patio. The morning dew had soaked into John's clothing. Most of his belongings were damp. Mark at least had the fore thought to bring some cardboard boxes to put his brothers' belongings in. He had expected to pack John's possessions, but not like this. They soon put everything in the van and drove off towards Paul and T's place they had a big garage to the side of their house, Ideal to store John's things. As Mark reversed the van up the drive to the garage, Paul appeared and opened the garage doors. It wasn't long before they were taking the last few boxes from the van. Paul put the last box down in the garage and said "Let's get in and have a drink, tea alright "Both Len and Mark nodded.

The next day John was looking around the dining room watching everyone. His eyes lit up when he noticed his brother Mark walking towards him. "Alright John!!" Mark said. "Hi Mark" said John smiling, pleased to see his brother. Mark said, "Why don't we go back to your room for privacy and chat there?" "Okay" said John looking a bit bemused. John sat on his bed Mark fetched a chair nearby and sat near John. Mark perked up "Yesterday Dad and I went to your house and picked up your clothes and your guitar's and thing's, we've stored it all at Paul and T's garage where it will be safe, so don't worry John your precious guitar's, are safe". John gasped and breathed out with relief. Mark said "The next thing is to find a place for you to live" John could see his brother had obviously thought about this. "What do you suggest" said John " What about the free papers, that's a start, where we can look through the ads and see what's about." Said Mark and John nodding his head in agreement. "OK" said John showing some enthusiasm. They both waded through the papers looking at the adds, nothing said Mark, John looked at Mark "Same here" John replied with disappointment written all over his face. Mark noticed; this is just the start John were try again on Thursday. John perked up a little and said "Okay, I've got the time and the patients" They both grinned at each other. "I'll bring Sue next time she'll help us" said Mark. "I've been in Hospital for 6 months on the 23rd of February that's 3 weeks away' 'John said. They both couldn't believe it's been so long.

Chapter 25

◆●◆

All the close family came to see John. Len, Joyce, T, Paul, Mark, and Sue rallied around John in the dining room, sitting around a large table, chatting away drinking tea and coffee. Gina turned up out of the blue not realizing they would all be there. "What do you want" Len said. "you've got a nerve; you have the audacity to come here now. Don't you think you've done enough damage" Len said angrily. " I have a letter here for John"? She said assertively. She walked over to John and placed the letter on the table in front of him, and then turned and walked towards the door and disappeared out to her car.

"It looks official" said Mark. John was curious as they all were. He gave it to T to open, and she opened it and passed the contents back to John, a letter. He looked at the letter reading it slowly to himself. He looked up; everybody was looking at him. "What is it son" Len said. John was a lot stronger now. "She's put in for Divorce' 'John said looking up at everybody, "she's really going for it what a cow bag." John said as they all looked at him in despair. Paul suddenly spoke up "You're better off without her John" all the family nodded and agreed looking at each other.

The following week Len and Joyce were allowed to take John out in the car and back to their house. John was loving it, Mum's cooking was the best, home cooked food ever, He thought. John made the most of his freedom, Mum spoilt him rotten. She cooked him a roast beef dinner with crispy roast potatoes and all the trimmings. When he couldn't eat any more, John asked if he could sit in the sitting room. "Course you can Son' 'Len said. Happy to have his son home. John sat on the sofa; the door was ajar. After 10 minutes both Len and Joyce peered around the door to see their son falling asleep, with his head tilted back. They both looked at each other without saying a word, grinning like two Cheshire cats. They left John to sleep for an hour then Joyce placed a cup of tea on the coffee table in front of John and gave him a light nudge on the shoulder with her hand. John came round "Oh god I fell asleep Mum sorry" wiping his eye's. "That's alright Son your father and I are pleased to have you home" she said with a twinkle in her eye. They all sat and chatted about old time's, John didn't remember a lot of what they were saying, but smiled and laughed, all in the right places. The next day, Mark and Sue came to see John at Alfred Morris, "We've got a surprise to show you John' 'said Mark as they walked out into the car park. Sue smiled to herself as she got into their car, they drove him back to their place, "What's this......this isn't your placc is it, really" John said. Amazed. "You live here Mark" John said staring at the house. "What about your flat" said John totally confused. "is this the surprise Mark" John still staring at the house. "John this is our house" Mark said looking at Sue, Sue smiled back at Mark. "Sue and I have bought this place, come on let's get inside and I'll show you round. Mark showed off his handy work, he just decorated the sitting room with real bold colours. John thought that's different but somehow it worked well with the curtain's the sofa and chairs. They had coffee and a sandwich in the kitchen, sitting on stools around the breakfast bar. Mark suggested they look at the local papers to find a place for John to live. For an hour they were sifting through the papers trying to find something suitable. "absolutely nothing at all" Mark said with a disappointed frown on his face "Me to, sorry John' 'Sue said scratching her head. "Well, something will come up soon I'm sure, I've been looking for myself, while in the Hospital, but no luck" John replied with disappointment written all over his face. Mark looked at his watch "It's nearly half past five, where did the day go, we best get you back to the hospital John, Sue gave John a hug and said "Were pop down to see you again John and don't worry, your find a place, I'm sure' 'she said smiling.

Mark drove John back to the Hospital dropped him off, making sure he was settled in OK. "Sue and I will see you soon

John, oh I didn't tell you, Sue and I are getting married next year" "What"? said John. "Why didn't you tell me earlier Mark" John looking happy and excited at the same time. "We can talk about it tomorrow John' 'Mark said with a grin on his face. Mark put his hand on John's shoulder and gave it a slight squeeze, he turned around and walked away down the corridor.

Chapter 26

◆◆ ● ◆◆

Doctor Shore was in Sister Sue Tiley's office, they were discussing John's improvement physically and mentally. Doctor Shore started the conversation looking down at John's notes. 'First of all, John is still having difficulty remembering words to describe thing's and express himself, obviously his vocabulary will improve with time, nevertheless the other concern is his mobility, He's weak down his right side. He's able to put his weight on his right leg, and support himself with a walking stick, but he can't walk very far and gets tired very quickly, but again that's to be expected and will improve over time." said Doctor Shore in thought and placing his thumb and index finger on his chin. Sue replied. " He's improving all the time, his walking skill's as you said will improve so will his vocabulary, I think we should see how he gets on with daily chores, to retain more independence, like making a hot drink?" "I agree" said Doctor Shore as his pager rang out. Doctor Shore stood up and put John's folder he was holding under his arm. "Keep me informed Sue Ok!" She agreed as he walked out her office closing the door behind him.

Another week went by, and John not only made tea, but cooked spaghetti bolognaise for himself and another patient who loved it. In fact, he came over in his electric wheelchair to the serving hatch for seconds, John was only to please for him to have a second helping. Things were moving at a fast pace, John looked through the papers and found a ground floor one bedroom flat in Bridgwater. He sat in his wheelchair in the foyer by the public phone that was set at wheelchair height, he rang the number in the paper The third ring a man answered the phone. "Hello" said the voice. John said "I was wondering if the flat is still available" With a keen tone in his voice. "Yes, it is" The man said. "I'll take it if that's Ok" John said. The man was surprised "You don't want to see it first and I haven't told you the rent" He exclaimed. "No" said John "I know the area, oh by the way my name's John." "really" the man said. "That's my name too" They both started to Laugh. "OK John when are you thinking of moving in". John told him his story and how he has spent 6 months in hospital. "Wow I didn't think a women could be that cruel, that's some story John, I bet you thank god you got through it"? " Well, I've been given a second chance to start, a new life, and that's what I'm going to do". The landlord John could feel the determination in his voice, "Look" He said "To save confusion call me by my middle name Norman my mother does. "Ok Norman it is"? John said.

John was released from Alfred Morris Rehabilitation Centre on the 23rd of February he spent 6 months in Hospital. When he was getting his things together to leave. He remembered telling Barry the male nurse that he was going to walk out of here. There's no sign of Barry, John thought, oh well. Joyce arrived with T's daughter Alison who was 6 years old, they both had a glee in their eyes and smiley faces. Joyce brought the wheelchair around to John's side of the bed. "Mum I said I was going to walk out of here" And he stood behind the wheelchair ready to push it. "OK Son, are you ready" Joyce said proudly. "Yes, let's do it' John replied. They put John's washing bag and the few clothes he had while he was in hospital on the seat of his wheelchair. John had already said his goodbyes to the other patients, Nurses and Doctors. They started walking out of the ward and down the corridor, it just seemed like any other day. No Barry oh well, John thought. As he walked nearer the foyer, he could see some nurses and doctors standing there chatting to one another. And before John could say anything they turned to face John, there was a great cheer and hand clapping. And John could see Barry in the crowd of uniforms cheering him on. Barry stepped out from the crowd and shook John's good hand "Well done John were all proud of you". John was overcome with emotion he tried to hold it in, his lower lip was trembling, and happy tear's fell down his cheeks, but he was smiling ear to ear at everyone. Joyce was holding back tears of joy, 6year old Alison looked puzzled. What's the big deal. She thought but cheered anyway.

They loaded the car and drove off down the road and onto the motorway to John's new home, they parked on the other side of the road where there were a couple of spaces left. "Let's go and see the flat first John" Joyce said as Alison held her Uncle John's hand and helped John across the road. She felt ever so grown-up holding Uncle John's hand. Let's wait for Nan" John said to Alison who looked up to her uncle John and smiled. Nan crossed the road. "What number is it John" Joyce said as she watched him pull out a piece of paper out of his pocket. "nineteen Mum" John said excitedly. "That's the next one along" said Joyce pointing with her finger. They all stood outside the front door; John knocked on the door. Norman the landlord was expecting them, John had phoned earlier. The door opened "Hello it's John isn't it, my names Norman, come inside I'll show you round the flat" He opened the door wider to let them in. "That way, the doors unlocked" he said, Norman shut the front door and walked past them all and spoke. "if you like to follow me, I'll show you the sitting room first. As they stood there, Norman looked at Joyce. She perked up and said "I'm John's Mother Joyce and this is my granddaughter Alison' 'she said He shook Joyce's hand and waved his fingers at the little girl, she went red and cuddle nan's leg, staring at him. "Along the corridor is the bathroom opposite is the bedroom and the kitchen is down the other end" Feel free to have a look around and I'll meet you back here" said Norman watching his P's and

Q's. He could see they were nice people, decent up standing. After a few minutes they walked back into the sitting room, John was last. It's just perfect for John, "It's not too far from the shop's" said John, with his head turning looking around "Those are old sash windows, do they open" John inquired. "No, they've been painted shut" Said Norman, "Oh Ok no worries" John said.

Chapter 27

T he flat was unfurnished, so John stayed with his parents for a few days, while his Dad Len organized some furniture to be delivered, a bed, cooker, fridge, washing machine all bought from a second-hand shop, and he arranged with the man to deliver the following day. Len was there early, a van pulled up outside, Len looked out the window, then went to the front door to let them in. As they unloaded and brought things into the flat, Len pointed to the two men where things should go. The last few things were a TV, sofa, dining table and two chairs. Len gave both men a fiver each for their trouble. "Thanks very much Sir" Both men replied, they left the flat and got in the van and drove off.

The day before, Len bought a Kettle, Crockery, Cutlery, and some saucepans and put it in the kitchen cupboards and drawers. He also bought some bedding and two pillows, and he looked around each room making sure he hadn't forgotten anything. No, were good to go, He thought to himself. Later that day Len came back to the flat with Joyce and John, John was excited yet a bit dubious about the whole thing, Joyce never said a word. She thought I'll make it a bit more homely, that's what it needs a women's touch, she thought. They parked up and hurried towards the front door, once they were inside, John and Joyce had a look around. "Thanks Dad this is great" John said walking into the sitting room. "A TV too" with a surprised look on his face. Joyce was in the bedroom making the bed up. Len said "Hang on son I've left something in the car" And hurried off. When he returned, he was carrying a plastic bag. "What's that dad" John said curiously. Len opened the bag to show his son the contents. "Here we are son your mother bought you the necessities, tea bags sweeteners and milk and four mugs." "Thanks Mum" John yelled! "That's Ok son" yelled Joyce, Busy making the bed.

Both Len and Joyce had a cup of tea with John and stayed for a while, now son you've got your mobile, any problems just phone. Len shook John's hand; Joyce came over and gave him a big hug and kissed him on the cheek. "You phone us if you need anything son" She put her hand on his shoulder to brush something away. "OK Mum don't worry, I'll be fine." Shortly after they had gone, peace and quiet John thought. He sat on the sofa and relaxed, he was content. Next thing the doorbell rang, he nearly jumped out of his skin, he'd not heard it before. He slowly got up and walked to the front door, he opened the door to find Gina standing there. "What do you want, and how did you know where I lived " he said annoyingly. "The Hospital told me." She said Looking all sweet and innocent. "Well, what do you want" John said not wanting to waste any more time with her. "I have the last lot of bills for the house, and this is from my solicitor to finalise the divorce" Gina shoved them into John's good hand forcefully grinning smugly. "The house is being repossessed, all the bills are in your name only, so it's your responsibility to pay them. Oh, the telephone bill is a little high because I had to ring around and cancel all the venues you were booked to play." She turned around and walked off. John still shocked, shut the door and walked back in the sitting room, clenching the envelopes in his hand. He sat down and started to open the Solicitor's letter first which he was expecting it was an appointment with the solicitor to sign the necessary papers for the divorce. Then the bills. Gas, Electricity, Water rates and finally the telephone bill, it amounted to quite a sum. John thought he'll have to pay these bill's off in instalments. He phoned the suppliers on his mobile and sorted it out. He explained his situation to all of them, who sympathized. He sat there thinking to himself, what am I going to do with the rest of my life. I must change my attitude. My marriage is finished I've lost my house thanks to Gina. I can't go back to work as a carpenter with my arm like it is. I can't play the guitar and after the tracheotomy, I can't sing either. His Mother had left a free newspaper on top the TV. John picked it up and placed it on the table and sat down to look, wading through the pages of adds, he came across a college add, open day next week. That's it, he thought to himself, I'll go to college. Little did he realize; it was the best thing he had done after leaving hospital. He went to the open day and spoke to staff and signed up for NVQ Level 1 Carpentry and Joinery and a beginner's course on Computer's. John explained his disability to college staff who were very helpful in organizing transport to and from his flat.

Time flew by, and September suddenly raised its head, John started College on the 7[th of] September on a Monday. He felt nervous, how many will be there, what is it going to be like, and a lot of other things went through his mind. He was picked up at 8.30 am and taken to college, he wasn't sure where he was supposed to go. The driver said "Go to the help desk and ask their mate" He pointed in the direction of the main entrance. "Okay thanks', 'said John. "somebody will be here to pick you up this afternoon" The taxi driver replied and pulled away, down the road. John walked inside and right up to the reception desk. "Excuse me' John said. The women behind the counter held up a finger at John, as if to say one minute, he hadn't realized she was on the phone via a Bluetooth earpiece. He waited, she turned to John and said "How can I help you" she said cheerfully and smiling. "I've signed up on a Carpentry course." Before he could say another word, the women said '' if you go back outside and turn right, follow the road around to the back of the main building your see a Carpentry and Joinery sign, you can't miss it, it's the big building on the left ok"! She smiled again at

John, he nodded with a cheeky grin.

When he got there, John went inside the building and there were other students of all ages, some sitting on the work bench's some standing. John mingled in amongst the students, the next thing a loud voice said "Can I have your attention please, my name is Andy Partridge I will be teaching all the practical side of Carpentry and Joinery for the next 2 years. today I will be explaining where everything is and the do's and don'ts in other words, Health and Safety while you're in the workplace. A few students mumbled and whispered to each other, "It's important you take all this in, because your life could depend on it" Andy said, hearing a couple of younger students sniggering. There was a coffee break at 10.30am, and they all like sheep followed each other to the canteen. They all sat on two large tables near each other and started introducing themselves. There were loads of students everywhere a lot of them had that lost look on their faces and didn't seem to know where they were going. The first day went well for John, he made some friends and he felt he was achieving something, doing something positive, he thought.

Chapter 28

◆●◆

The next day John was picked up by taxi and dropped off at the same place in college. He walked to the canteen; His walking had improved slightly. He was still swinging his leg and locking his knee to put his weight on it, but with more confidence. He agreed to meet 3 older students in the canteen, the day before. The three of them were already there sitting drinking tea. They'd saved John a seat, "How's it going "John said. They all nodded "It's Darrell, Paul and Neri is that right' 'John said not very confidently. "That's right" said Darrell. "Take a seat" "well I'll just get a cup of tea first, how long have we got till class" said John putting his shoulder bag down next to his chair. "Don't worry we've got plenty of time yet" Paul said laughing while students were passing in all directions like an ant's nest.

They all got on with the theory and practical, John struggled sometimes with holding certain tools like a plane, in the workshop. The guys would see him struggling and offer to help, time went by and the next thing it was end of the first term. John got dropped home to his flat, he thanked the driver and went inside. The night before he cooked one of his favourites, Cottage Pie. That's tea sorted he thought, might stroll up to the Lime Tree pub just up the road, for a couple of pints later with a smile on his face. He'd gone up there a few times before, the couple who ran the place George and Lyn, husband, and wife. They were quite chatty, and they were quite taken with John, and got to know him quite well. They occasionally had live music, which of course John loved. He wasn't too keen on the amount of people pushing and shoving at the bar as he was still a bit shaky on his feet, he would take his walking stick for stability.

Len thought he'd take the opportunity and go and visit Gina's parents, who lived a little outside of town. Joyce refused to go as she was still upset with their daughter-in-law. Len sat in his car, signed, and took a deep breath, then started the car. He thought if he dropped in on Gina's parents to see how the land lies with the fact, That Gina had filed for divorce while John was still in Hospital and losing the house after the accident. Did they have any idea about all this, and what was happening now he wondered. But he was about to find out, he scratched his head and drove off. He parked his car outside of their house and sat there for a moment and caught his breath. He prepared himself. He knew Martin and Jackie were quiet and kept themselves to themselves, so he wasn't so much preparing for an argument or fight but he was preparing to let everything out of his system. He rang the doorbell and from inside he could hear children running to answer the door. "I'll get it Nan". Len's heart started beating faster. Could it be, he wondered? Could it be that Jason and little Brad were here".?

Len could hear Jason say "I'll get it Nan"! And Brad followed him "Hurry up Nan!" Jason said all excited and inpatient as he waited for his Nan to open the door. The door opened and the two boys rushed out and fell into Len's open arm's as he bent down. Jason and Brad hugged him tight. "I've missed you two guys' so much and Nanny has to' 'said Len. Len stood up and patted their heads as they both stepped back inside the house, brushing passed their Nan. "Hello Jackie" said Len. Martin popped his head around the door to see who it was. "Hello Len, it's been a long time" Martin said all surprised. "Come in, Len" he said with a welcoming smile, Jackie opened the door wider to let him in. "What a nice surprise to see you" said Martin shaking his hand, is Joyce alright, how is she keeping" Martin said genuinely. "She's very well thanks"? Martin straightens his arm pointing it to the kitchen "Go on through Len" Martin said still gesturing with his arm. Len passed him and through to the kitchen, Jackie and Martin followed.

Jackie filled the kettle and placed it on its stand. The boys had disappeared in the sitting room playing with some toy's

Martin had left out earlier. A few minutes went by, then Jason walked into the kitchen and looked at Len, ''Grandad'' he said "We haven't seen Daddy for a long time' 'Jason pulled a sad face. "Yes, I know son he misses you guy's very much" said Len. "Why hasn't he been to see us said Jason frowning, Len put his hand on his chin and rubbed it, looking at Martin and Jackie and then looked back at Jason, both didn't have a clue. "You have to ask your mummy about that Jason" said Len looking at Martin and Jackie again. "You go play in the sitting room with your brother and don't worry, your see Daddy soon, I promise." Jason smiled and ran back to his brother. "What's this all about Len" Martin said getting straight to the point. "It's your daughter she's been a right nasty piece of work" Len said getting louder. Jackie shut the kitchen door so the boys wouldn't hear, "Look Len, Gina came out to see us with the boys and broke down, we thought with John in Hospital and all that, was the reason." "No" said Len "She wanted you to have the boys for the weekend, so she could meet her boyfriend and stay over at his place for the weekend." "What" said Martin "Are you serious' 'He gasped.

Jackie stood behind her husband "She wouldn't do that' 'Jackie said putting her hand over her mouth. "All the time John was in Hospital and no doubt before, your daughter was messing about, while John worked hard to support her and the kids" Len banged his fist on the table in rage, spilling tea from the mugs. "You really don't know what your daughter is capable of, do you." "That's enough you've overstayed your welcome

Len, I'll walk you to the door" said Martin thinking about his step daughter she loved John she wouldn't do anything like that, he's got it all wrong, he thought. Martin marched Len to the door, Len shouted "Bye boys see you soon" Jackie opened the sitting room door so the boys could say goodbye to their Grandad, "Bye Grandad" both boy's shouted from the front door as Len walked down the drive.

John was thinking about the boys throughout College, Gina stopped him from seeing them quite awhile ago. As if she hadn't hurt him enough. He acted through a solicitor to see his boys; Gina was being a right cow. After nearly three months of waiting it finally went to court, the judge decided, John could have his boys one weekend and one Saturday a month. It was a relief for John to finally see his boys, the first time he saw them, Gina dropped them off at his home. John bent down on one knee at the end of the path ready to give them a big hug they were so pleased to see him.

Over the weekend John took them to the play area across from where he lived. They both stayed with there dad, one each side. Allowing their dad to walk at his pace with his walking stick, they seemed to understand their dad's disability. Watching them play football reminded john when he took them to the park and played footie with them. He pushed brad on a swing, Jason was very independent he didn't need any help. They all had a great time together. Gina turned up Sunday afternoon to pick them up. "Ahh mum can't we stay with daddy a little bit longer" both staring at their mother with sad eye's. "no. get your thing's and say goodbye to your dad" Gina said as if she had to be somewhere else. Gina stuck with this arrangement through out. It was coming up to 3 years at college, John had completed his evening class one day a week on a Wednesday night, it was for his CITB 6111 NVQ Level 1 in Construction. He did manage to get a lift from another student who lived up the road from him. Plus, during his college courses, he made a lot of new friends. And being full time at college his week was full of classes both practical and theory. He was hungry for knowledge and there was plenty of it. John completed 3 years at College, and he passed NVQ Level 1 & 2 in Carpentry and Joinery, City and guilds 1 & 2 in furniture making, he even managed to pass the Pre-vocational Exam in Carpentry and Joinery, with the institute of Carpenter's. The final fourth and fifth year John took another direction, as well as finishing his Carpentry and furniture making, he started some courses on Computers full time. He'd already taken computer courses part time throughout the past three years of carpentry and joinery.

For the next 2 years John did full time courses from Pascal computer programming, Database, Spreadsheets, power point and desktop publishing. From there he carried on with office skills, Computer literacy and RSA text processing, IBT level 2 and build your PC. He finished his 5th year, in that time John had moved to another property not to far from the College. a week after he moved in, the council got a contractor to put a cubicle shower in place of the bath, they fitted the shower in one day, that made life a lot easier for john.

He found out that he could get a car from motability, and they could adapt it for him to drive. He made some inquiries at the ford showroom and garage in town, Neri a fellow student gave him a lift. John went through all the forms and everything. He picked the car upfitted with a steering knob and drove off the fore court onto the road and home. He was so pleased with himself, I'm mobile he thought. I could pick the boy's up myself that will be a kick in the teeth for Gina he thought and smiled to himself.

A couple of weeks went by, it was Friday, he'd finished college for the weekend, and
drove into town. parked near the library in a disabled space. As he was walking, he bumped into an old friend or should I say she approached him and said "hello john how are you" he looked at her and thought do I know you, he couldn't remember, looking all confused. She took the time to explain to John that her name was Debbie they met in a pub in town years ago. This was before John was married, they chatted for awhile and agreed to meet for a coffee the next day.

John was early, he walked into the Bridge cafe and sat by the window. He thought she can't miss him sitting by the window by the entrance, well that's if she turns up, he thought. A little later there she was a little half-hearted wave with her hand, John acknowledged by lifting his hand off the table and straightening his fingers. He stood up as she approached him "Let me get you a coffee or tea" he said smiling. "ok " Debbie said "I'll have a cappuccino with one sweetener please" and sat down. "the waitress will bring it over in a minute" john said as he sat down. "So, tell me how do you know me deb's apart from meeting in a pub in town" john said curiously. The waitress brought her coffee over and placed it on the table in front of her "thank you" she said looking at the young girl and smiled, john noticed her gentle and polite manner. She started to explain to john how she saw him play in several places and enjoyed his music. "In fact, I thought you were really good" She said "honestly" john said surprised "honestly" she said. "You heard about the accident, you must of"? John said "ya that was a shock how are you doing now, I noticed you have a limp' 'she said. John raised his weak arm and it started to shake uncontrollably and said, ''I wouldn't shave with this arm" they both laughed. "When I left Hospital, I thought what could I do, I'm not the type to sit about, and so I signed up for college and ended up doing five years'"? "wow" she said with a look of surprise on her face? "What have you been doing there". She said looking puzzled.

"Well after the accident, not only was I physically disabled, having to learn to walk again, but I was psychologically disabled too. I had to learn to talk, read and write again I can't, remember how to play the guitar, well only some basic chords that's it." "Wow sounds like you've been through the mill john, ahh she said remembering he was married with two boys, what's your wife's name". She flicked her fingers frantically in the air, she paused thinking, placing her hand on her forehead aah. "Gina that's her name.... what does she say about all this " she said anxiously? "Ya Gina, divorced me while I was still in hospital, she said I was only half a man" he said picking up his coffee and taking a sip. "that's terrible how could she do that, that's really heartless" said Debbie. They swapped numbers and Email's and promised to meet up again soon.

Chapter 29

◆◆●◆◆

John was up early, showered and dressed, it was Saturday morning he just made himself a cup of tea and sat down in the kitchen. Suddenly the doorbell rang; he walked to the front door and opened it, to see his old mate Andy standing there. "Hello matey what's up' 'said John who stood back to let him in "I've just made a drink do you want one" John said cheerfully. "Ya I will thanks" Andy replied. John had known Andy for along time and could tell he had something on his mind. "What is it matey"? John asked. They both sat round the kitchen table, Andy took a sip of his tea and put his mug back down on the table and spoke. "what about getting back to playing again like we used to"? "Are you serious"? John said with a look of disbelieve, "what about Steve have you spoken to him yet". "No" said Andy, I was thinking of just you and I as a duo, Steve's wife has just had a baby so he won't have the time now, what do you think' 'John spoke up "how can we do that I can't play guitar and my voice, well I don't know what that would sound like after that tracheotomy thingy they put down my throat' 'John said looking bewildered. Andy looked at John and said "What if I come over to yours every day and we rehearsed I'll work out what key's suit you and we can work out what range you have and perhaps get you singing again, what do you say"? John looked at him, amazed he could suggest such a thing, but he was excited about the challenge and the thrill of getting back to singing again? John said "I think your mad, but let's go for it matey"? They picked up their mugs and put them together. They rehearsed every evening for a month, Andy managed to work out different keys on his guitar that John could sing comfortably with. They ordered backing tracks of songs on midi disk, that they used to do before, in the right key, and rehearsed some more. It wasn't long before they sounded pretty good, in fact it boosted john's confidence no end. Andy said "It sounds good John, what do you think"! "Your right I can't believe it, I'll have to buy a stool to sit on, I can't stand for an hour each time, it's too much" john paused for a minute. "what are we going to call are self's"? Andy said "what about 'Free Beer' they both laughed. Andy said "what about 'Last Chance' after your accident I think that's quite fitting, what do you think"? He said to John. "I think that's a great name, ok let's get a gig some where". John said feeling positive. Later that day john phoned some agencies that used to book them, they said there wasn't any thing now. What they really meant to say is, we heard about your accident, and we don't have any confidence in you performing anymore. That upset John all the effort both Andy and John had made. The phone suddenly rang "Hello" john said. "It's Andy, I got us a gig" he said excitedly. "that's great matey" john said regaining his confidence and grinning ear to ear. "Where is it" john asked. "your never guess, that pub up the road from your old flat, what's it called" Andy said. "What the lime tree" john said. "Ya that's the one"! "Oh no pressure then" john said jokingly. Before long it was Saturday the day of the gig, John and Andy were photographed and interviewed by three local papers, two weeks before at john's place. So, the gig was well advertised. Andy pulled up outside john's place and reversed up the drive, it was 6.30pm and as he got out the car, john was already waiting at the door, half opened. They both loaded the car up and shut the back of Andy's car.

They were all set up in the pub, everything was ready. People who new john had read in the papers that they were doing there first gig there. Two couples walked over to john doing some last minute checks on the mixer. "Hi john, your first gig" john turned around "hay guy's nice to see you" putting his hand out to shake their hands. "don't tell me" john said. "it's Samantha, ash, Steve and Sarah"! "that's right john, your memory getting better" said Steve. As the night progressed, the pub was filling up and knee deep at the bar. There were couples dancing and having a great time, one or two girls dancing together and looking over at john smiling. John looked at Andy grinning then looked back at the girls. John hadn't felt like this in a long time, it was a good feeling, he thought to himself. They started the last set with some rock and roll, the place was packed. John and Andy gave it there all. They slowed things down halfway through and couples got on the dance floor smooching together holding hands. Someone caught john's eye, a face at the back, he couldn't quite make out who she was. She stepped forward it was Debbie she winked at john, he couldn't believe it she'd come to see him play, john turned to Andy and said, " do this one on your own matey". Andy nodded he'd seen john looking at debs. John walked over to her took her hand and they danced as if they had danced many times before. He kissed her on the lips, before Andy had finished the song; he hurried back to his mic and stool. John looked back at Debbie and winked his eye, she smiled. The place was buzzing, they already played over time and the crowd were wanting more. George from behind the bar, the landlord looked over at john, he put his index finger in the air at john. John turned to Andy one more matey. They finished the night; they still wanted more. What a night john thought feeling really pleased with himself. He looked over at deb's she smiled as she walked over. "you haven't lost it john, giving him a kiss, what a night it's been she said. "Look I know you need to pack up everything so I'll go home, would you ring me tomorrow" she said. ''Of course, " john said unplugging cables. He stepped out from behind the mic stand and kissed her. "I'll phone you tomorrow I promise love. He watched her leaving, she turned and smiled at him as she left, john smiled back.

He phoned Deb's the next day, they had a good natter and laughed about one guy last night falling over after he drank to much, he spilled all his beer down his front it looked as if he'd wet himself, they both laughed. She spoke. "We'll have to meet up again soon John."? She emphasized. He agreed and said "See you soon Deb's take care......Bye" they both hung up

John and Andy carried on gigging once or twice a week, usually Friday's and Saturday's. They were enjoying the fun the excitement, the thrill of it all, and getting paid for it to. It was just like the old day's John thought. In the meantime, the council phoned John and offered him a ground floor flat in a village, where Paul and T lived, it had two bedrooms. He drove out and met the housing officer and was shown round the flat and he decided to take it. The following month John was due to move in, he'd been out nearly every day before as the housing officer Jane gave John the keys. Paul and T helped him bright, and early most mornings, John, Paul, and T were there in the flat, Paul putting up batten above the windows to hang curtain rails then putting up nets for privacy they hired a box van and managed to fill the van with all of John's furniture and belongings even the garden shed. They drove and parked outside the flat and unloaded everything, placing things in the appropriate rooms. John drove out to the flat most days doing little jobs that he could manage before the move, Paul painted walls put up curtain rails connected the electric cooker and other jobs before John moved in, T was out in the kitchen putting pots, pans

cutlery and crockery away, she already filled the kettle with water, put out three mugs and a teaspoon on the work top and brought tea bags, sweeteners and
some milk, she put in the fridge, from home.

Len and Joyce turned up out of the blue, Joyce got to work immediately making the bed up " Have these sheets been washed John" She said waiting for an answer. John was busy making tea for everybody. "Do you take a sweetener T" John shouted. "YES, please she answered. Joyce walked into the kitchen where John was and put some bedding in the washing machine. "That's clean Mum" John said as he looked round. "It smells a bit musky' 'She said putting it in the washing machine. She got hold of some other bedding and made the bed up, then plumping up the pillows so they'd look bigger and thicker.

Paul and T came along later to see how he was doing. It was a Wednesday, feeling pleased with himself. He walked around his new a bold, it looks nice and clean and smelt fresh, Paul had painted some of the walls in one or two rooms, I'll have to change those curtains in my bedroom they clash with the bedding, and I want laminate flooring in there as well? What am I saying, I sound like an old women? "Blimey get a grip son" he thought to himself. He went into town and did a shop, stocked up the fridge and got a few things for the freezer. He sat in the sitting room on his favourite leather reclining chair sipping the cappuccino he'd just made.

Chapter 30

◆◆●◆◆

Later that evening he took his walking stick and wondered down the church path to the back of the old Pub. He opened the door and stepped into a hallway, opposite was another door he opened it not sure where it went, to find himself in the lounge bar. Being new to the village all heads turned to look at John, he felt they were analyzing him from top to toe. That was a bit weird he thought. They soon settled down and went back to what they were doing, drinking, and chatting.

He stood at the bar, the barmaid was a middle-aged woman, with long brown wavy hair and a kind caring face. "good evening what would you like" she said.

I'll have a Pint please" Pointing at one of the pumps. She started pouring his pint "not seen you here before' 'She said. "No, I've just moved into the village, what's your name" said John with an inquisitive smile, as she placed his pint on the bar. John picked his drink up taking a sip and handing her a tenner. "I'm Bev' 'she said. "My names John. John Blackmoore, my sister and her husband live in the village" he said. "oh really" said Bev walking back from the till and handing him his change.

"What goes on in the village" John asked taking another sip. "Just one minute" she said. Hearing some commotion in the back bar. Two young lads were arguing about something. "I'll be back in a minute John" she said wondering off. The noise soon quieten down, he looked around and thought this is an old pub. Wall lights, Low ceilings with beams and with old, framed pictures of men and women working on the land hanging on the walls. Turning right around there was an old open fireplace, with copper pots and brasses hanging from the walls and ceiling. I bet that's nice and warm in the winter he thought. Bev came back "where were we" she said. "I was asking you about the village and what goes on here." Oh yes, getting back to her trail of thought. The community centre gets used for all sorts, from bingo, dances, live music." John's ears stood up. "Live music"! He said a bit to loud, as people looked over at him. John looked around at them grinning submissively. " We have the Sealed Knot once a year, 'what's that? John said. Bev took a breath. "It's a group of volunteers of all ages re enacting the battle of sedge-moor on the original ground where it took place". "Really' 'he paused." surprised. "Ya really, it goes on all day, and they finish up here, didn't you know that" She said. She also went on to say. "This battle was the last battle fought on British soil' 'looking straight at John, to see his reaction. "wow" he said all surprised. "I only came down for a pint, I didn't expect to get a history lesson too' 'He laughed, Bev grinned.

"What's the Landlord called here Bev" John being inquisitive. " Richard and Melanie, they run the place"! "What are they like"? John inquired. "They are nice people John, there from the village". "Oh ok" John replied.

He settled into village life and went down the pub quite often, getting to know the locals. One night the landlord Richard was behind the bar. He went over to John, who was sitting in the corner of the bar and said I hear your in a band? "No" John said "There's only two of us". And smirked. We sound like a band because we use backing tracks on a Midi disk player"! John replied. "You've lost me, I'm hopeless when it comes to technology" Said Richard looking slightly vacant. "What about doing a gig here one night"? Richard said looking at John. John's face lit up followed by a big smile. "Ya, I'd love to, when?" Said John. "What about three weeks time on a Saturday" Richard said putting his pen in his mouth then turning pages in his diary.

John said. "I'll have a word with my mate Andy and get back to you, is that alright"?

"Sure, let us know as soon as you can John" Said Richard. John phoned Andy the following day to confirm the booking, It was all arranged. Mean time John had the boys for the weekend, it was special because the sealed knot re enact the battle of

Sedgemoor. John took the boys to the field behind the community centre where the battle commenced after marching through the village. John bought both boys a burger each, and they stood there watching all these people, all dressed up as peasants or soldiers with long lances. Both boys were busy eating their burgers, when suddenly there was this loud bang. They'd just fired a canon near by, both boys jumped nearly losing the burgers. It frighten little Brad he walked over to his dad for reassurance. "It's ok little man it's all part of the fun" said John, Bradley grinned with relief, taking a bite out of his burger. Jason didn't worry he's like his dad it would take more than that to frighten him. It was getting near teatime, so John and the boy's walked back to his place. He had cooked earlier that day. "What's for eats Dad" said Brad sounding a bit tired. "I've made spaghetti Bolognese." "Oh great" said Jason with a big smile on his face and An appetite to match, he loved his dad's cooking. They all sat at the table and tucked in, John had bought a French stick which he cut up and buttered and put on a plate on the table, and in no time the guys were all full. Later that evening they all sat on the sofa and watched a DVD it was a comedy, they all laughed and messed about, eating popcorn, and drinking coke. The film had finished, it was getting late so John got the boys to get their PJ's on and clean their teeth. Both boys got into bed, and it wasn't long before they were asleep.

It was Sunday, John had to take the boys back to there Mother by 5PM. Well guy's lets go for a drive and maybe stop for lunch somewhere on the way. "Great" said Jason, Brad was preoccupied playing his Nintendo. John drove out to a little village pub, in the car park were four guys', sat on hay bells on the back of An old wooden cart, playing jazz. A lot of people were sitting outside, having a drink and listen to the music. John and the boy's got back in the car and drove a bit further. They stopped at the next pub, which looked family friendly. There were swings and slides and kids running about, this looks alright John thought. They stopped and had some lunch, "Dad" said Jason "what son" John replied. "Can I have a dessert; I will eat it dad I promise" said Jason. Brad perked up "me to Dad, Ill eat it all to". "Ok guy's what do you want." Both boys ate their entire dessert and washed it down with coke. "Come on guys I better take you back to your mothers it's twenty past four" Said John.

John had bought himself a desktop computer, printer, and scanner awhile ago, to help him with his college work. He also used it to regularly chat to people all round the world. He spoke to one person called Becky from the USA, who taught business studies in a college in Delaware. One night they were chatting away, and Becky said. "Johnny I'm planning a trip to a friends wedding in Sweden next month, what about if I arrange to fly to the UK and get a train to Somerset and see you for a few days, what do you say"? John looked at his screen surprised and spoke. "Sure, that would be great becks." He was surprised yet excited all in one. They'd been chatting on the computer to each other for over a year.

Chapter 31

◆◆●◆◆

Saturday came along, the day of the gig, The Landlord; Richard advertised live music in the parish magazine, which was the village news paper, two weeks before. he was expecting a good turn out. John and Andy set there gear up in the back bar in front of the dart board. Both sides the lounge and the bar started to fill up, with local people. A lot of them knew John from the village, there were a few people John hadn't seen before. The night went well everybody dancing and drinking. It was getting late so John announced on the mic, "Well I hope you've had a good night, guy's we have, were going to slow it down or should I say Andy is going to, with a nice slow number, take it away Andy". John went out from behind the mic and mingled while Andy sang and played guitar with the backing. A woman was looking at John he noticed, she had long blonde hair and a lovely figure, he walked over and said would you like a dance she nodded her head and said "sure". They danced and near the end John asked her name "Liz" she said. "ok Liz thanks for the dance" John said and he managed to get back just in time. "Andy" John said Let's finish off with are favourite" Andy nodded. John announced "this is the last one guy's hope we see you all again" and they went straight into the last number everybody got up and danced, foot tapping and drinking. We finished finally after 5 more numbers, and they still wanted more. Richard the Landlord looked over at John and shook his head. "Okay everybody that's its good night." There were loud whistling, shout's for more and One guy came over with his pint in his hand saying "come on just one more" He said in drunken desperation then gave up and went back to the bar. John and Andy were busy packing up to notice the guy. People in the village seemed to treat John differently after the gig, in the village shop and the pub, they treated him with a little respect.

John was chatting to Becky online one night and Becky said. "It's the Soccer world series and the yacht club are doing, pull a piece of paper out of a hat with a team on it for $25.00 winner takes all. Do you want to have ago" she said? "What does that mean" John said a little confused. "It's the soccer world series here in the states Johnny and if your team win, I'm not sure how much yet, but you will get more than $25.00. "Could you put $25.00 down for me and I will sort the money out with you later if that's alright." Becky didn't hesitate "sure" she said. She kept on to John about flying over the pond. "Look Beck's I don't know if I could sit on a plane for over 7 hours or more. I have flown before, but not for that long, and that was before my accident, and I can't remember what it was like. "Johnny, I'll pick you up at the airport no worries, it's only two-and-a-half-hour drive to Philadelphia airport" She said as if it were a drive into town and back. "ok I'll make some inquires online and in town tomorrow" John said not believing he'd just said that. "You'll have a great time here Johnny" She said. It was a few days later Becky got in touch with John on his PC. It was early evening as she was 5 hours behind. "Johnny, Johnny you won" she said John with his memory couldn't remember he told her to put $25.00 bet on the world series. "You won" again she said excited. John said "won what"? With an odd looking expression on his face. "Have you forgotten already" Beck's said bewildered. "You won $500.00 Johnny, now your have to come over here to pick it up"? She smirked at the screen.

She could hear John making all sorts of noises and shouting "Yes back of the net'.

"Johnny' 'she said again. John sat down and said to her "I never win anything, this is great and yes; I will come over and see you Beck's and thank you so much for winning".

"Johnny, you won not me. well done I'm pleased you're flying over the pond" She was happy for him and happy he was coming over to stay for a holiday.

She was true to her word; she flew to Sweden to her friends wedding and then flew into Heath-row airport London a week later. From there she took a train to Taunton in Somerset, where she arranged for John to pick her up in his car. It took about 35 minutes to get home, John helped her carry her luggage into his flat. He showed her the boys room, "I know it's small with bunk beds" he said. "Johnny its ok, I'll be fine"? He showed her around the rest of the flat so she would be familiar with the surroundings.

That evening John took Becky down the church path and into the pub. They both stood at the bar, Bev appeared from the back bar, "Hi Bev" said John" This is my friend Becky from the USA" with a grin on his face. Becks said "Hi" John ordered the drinks; Becky had a pint of lager and John had his usual beer. Becky said "I haven't eaten since this morning and I'm starving". She asked Bev if they did food. Bev handed her a menu, they both had steak medium rare. Becky followed John and they sat down, she told John how the wedding went in Sweden and how friendly the people were. She looked around and said "this place is old" still looking around. I know Beck's I think it's 6 or 700 years old". "WOW" She said. "Love that fireplace" smiling while she pointed. I know I told you this before, the last battle on English soil was fought here, he paused thinking about it. "It was 6th July 1685. Pleased with himself that he remembered. They tucked into there steaks and had a couple more pints while they chatted.

The next day John drove Beck's into town, parked by the river and they both walked up the high street, stopped for a cake and coffee in the Bridge Cafe. John asked her if she wanted to do anything. She said "I'm quite happy with what you want to do Johnny" She said contently. Becks looked in the window of a few shops, nothing of interest and then they both walked back to the car. John was thinking why don't I introduce her to my parents? He thought. So, he drove out to their place, Dad will be in the garden, Mother in the kitchen, he thought to himself. Ya just as he thought, he pulled up behind his dad's car and got out, Becky followed. "Hi Dad" he said. His dad was already walking over to greet his passenger. Dad this is Becky from the states, he put his hand out, they shook hands, "my names Len. Becky what a lovely name' 'He said. "Well, thank you " Becky replied. "come and meet my wife" said Len Gesturing towards the side door of the bungalow. "Hay love" Len called" as he stepped inside "where are you girl"? He turned to Becky and said "she's about somewhere"! Joyce suddenly appeared from nowhere. "I heard you calling love." wiping her hands in a tea towel and a pinnie around her waist. "Oh" she said hugging John. " are you alright son and who is this" she said looking at Becky. "this is Becky my friend from the states' 'John replied. Joyce stepped forward and gave her a hug, Becky was surprised with such a welcome and wasn't used to being hugged, but she gave it a go. She thought John's parents were very nice and genuine people.

They ended up stopping for the afternoon, Len and Joyce were asking Becky all sorts of questions about the states, her horses and what she did in College, Becky took it in her stride. Three cups of Tea with biscuits and sandwiches, Joyce always new how to treat her guest's. They stood by the front door, you must visit again Becky, Joyce hugged her, Len shook her hand. Come here son and gave him a big hug and kissed him on the cheek. "You look after Becky son" she said "I will Mum" John replied. Both Len and Joyce waved as they drove off, "I like Becky" said Joyce, Len agreed as he shut the door.

The four days flew by, and the next thing John was taking Becky back to the railway station. They both stood on the platform not saying anything, waiting for the train, "well Beck's I'm going to book a flight to the states in the next couple of days and pay for it, so then I'll have to go" he said. "Make sure it's the end of June beginning of July Johnny" Becky replied assertively. "I will no problem" John said as the train pulled into the station.

Becky was used to it by now and gave John a hug which took John by surprise. "See you on the other side of the pond soon, 'Becky said looking straight at John smiling. "You will Beck's I promise" He was upset she was leaving but, in his eyes, he was determined, she could see how he felt and hugged him again. "Chat to you online when I get back home Johnny" She said boarding the train.

John couldn't see Beck's on the train, yet he raised his hand and waved to the train as the whistle sounded and the train started to move.

Becky used John's Computer before they left, to book a hotel in London for the night. Her flight was early the following morning. As soon as she got home, she Emailed John to let him know she got home safely.

Chapter 32

◆●◆

John did do what he said to Becky, he did book up and paid for the trip to the states. Coach to Heath-row then fly out to Philadelphia airport, where Beck's said she'd pick him up.

He did one or two more gigs with Andy and after 2 year's they both decided to call it a day. John sold his semi acoustic and his electric guitar plus the speakers and mixer, he thought why keep something that he wouldn't use.

Andy would quite often visit John at his flat in the village, have a chat over coffee, sometimes John cooked a meal. They always had a laugh at one or the other's expense, that's how it went.

That day came, there was no turning back, John had paid for the trip and there was no refund, he had to go. He was up early, showered and dressed, had a cup of tea and toast, while he was checking he had everything. Passport, Money, Toothbrush, toothpaste razors, shaving foam. He was starting to panic when the doorbell rang

It was Irene his friend who was going to take him to the bus station in town. "Hi are you ready." She said calmly. "Don't get yourself all wound-up John, there's no need" Said Irene looking at him all sympathetically. They loaded the car and headed into town, when they got there the driver was already loading cases on to the coach. They both stood there, looking at each other. "You have a good time John" said Irene a bit tearful, as if she wasn't going to see him again. John gave her a hug and kissed her. " I'm sort of looking forward to it now, not sure about the flying, but I've got to do it." He said biting his lip. He gave Irene another hug and boarded the coach, he could see Irene from his window seat. The driver got on the bus and started counting the passengers. "Yep, that's right" He said to himself lifting his cap and scratching his head. John gave Irene a slow wave has the coach pulled away; Irene smiled at him.

It seemed to take for ever, John needed the loo and there always seemed to be someone getting there before him. He thought if I don't stand by the door, I'll never get to use it. He stood there hanging on to a seat, with his good hand, the door opened a middle-aged women appeared holding the door for John as she could see he found it difficult to stand while the coach was moving. "Thank you very much" he said to her, she smiled and went back to her seat.

The coach drove into Heathrow airport and pulled up and parked alongside a dozen or more coaches all unloading cases for there passengers, who were waiting in groups by each coach and grabbing their cases as they appeared. At this point John was wondering where the help was, as he told the travel agent he needed assistants, as he couldn't walk to far, especially with his luggage. He had no choice but to struggle, he managed to get to the booking in area. He told the young man behind the counter that he asked the travel agent to organize transportation of some sort, as he couldn't walk to Far., He told him he was exhausted and needed help. The young man got on the phone for awhile and then hung up, looking at John he said. "I've organized some assistance for you, if you liked to sit and wait over there, sir, giving John his ticket, someone will be along shortly". He said with a cheerful smile. John nodded and tried to smile slightly "Thank you" Said John. It wasn't long before a young guy with a wheelchair, introduced himself and said he would take John to the departure lounge.

Eventually John got on the plane; he sat down in the seat he booked. Which was an end seat middle row to the right. He booked this seat so he could stretch his right leg, so he wouldn't have to keep standing up. It turned out to be a bad choice for John, as the two young guy's that sat next to him, were totally ignorant and oblivious to John's disability. Each time the guy who sat in the middle wanted to go loo, he disturbed John as the other guy would make out, he was asleep. So John was getting up and down throughout the flight, and it didn't help that the guy was drinking beer and vodka and cokes. As well as that a hostess gave John a form to fill out, it was a visa to enter the united states. She offered to help, and she did, that made life a lot easier for John. He thanked her for her help. She smiled as if she'd done it many times before.

The Captain came on the P.A. "We will be arriving at Philadelphia airport in 20 minutes; I hope you've had a pleasant flight please be seated and fasten your seat belts thank you". Thank god, John thought another hour with this joker beside him and he would blow a gasket.

He went through customs, then there were what looked like a row of podiums with gaps between them. John walked up to one of them. Stood behind the podium was a coloured policeman armed and very serious expression on his face. "Passport please" He said abruptly. John handed it over, he scanned the passport with his eye's then looked at John "is this trip business or pleasure sir." "Pleasure" John replied trying to swallow a lump in his throat, being so nervous. "Where will you be staying" he asked. "I'm staying with a friend" John said showing him Becky's address on a piece of paper. After a few minutes he stamped John's passport and handed it back to him. "Have a nice vacation sir" smiling at John. All John was thinking about was thank god for that, what a terrifying experience.

There was still no assistance with his luggage, so John had to take his case off the conveyer belt himself, which was a struggle, as it was constantly moving. Then he walked, following the flow of people, which took him to the arrivals area. People were being greeted with handshakes, hugs, and kisses, John kept looking around for Beck's he couldn't see her. Did she forget or did he give her the wrong day, he was starting to get flustered? Then suddenly a hand wave caught his eye, he looked a bit closer, it was Beck's. The relief on John's face as it suddenly bloomed into a big smile as he headed towards her. "Hi Beck's" John said giving her a hug of relief.

"How was your trip" said Becky. "A nightmare" said John as he explained to her about the two guy's who sat next to him on the plane.

It was 9pm by the clock on the wall, so John changed his watch accordingly, he followed Beck's to the automatic doors. When they opened the heat in the air hit John right in the face. It was just like the tropic's he thought, they carried on walking towards the car park. They were in the car on the highway in no time, two-and-a-half-hour drive. John thought 'thank god beck's car had air con or it would have been unbearable.' They drove off the highway and went down a country road and then Beck's turned left into a drive and right up to the front door of this big house, it was dark but there were lights on around the property. They got out, John could hear dogs barking from inside, don't worry Beck's said they don't bite. John followed Beck's into the house with his case, the dogs went straight to John barking and sniffing him. John put out his hand. "They are Labradoodles" Beck's said heading for the kitchen. They were like black curly haired great Dane's. John kept his hand out and they both started to lick John's hand, he ruffled the hair on there heads, and they lapped it up. Becks was in the kitchen "Are you hungry Johnny" She said. "No but I could do with a beer Beck's, I haven't had one for 2 days, and in this heat, I need one" He said dropping his case and shoulder bag to the floor heading towards the kitchen. John walked in the kitchen the dogs followed he sat down at the kitchen table, Beck's stuck her head in the huge fridge and turned round with a bottle of beer in her hand. "There you go Johnny one cold beer" She twisted the top off with her hand and gave it to him, Becky smiled watching him take his first mouthful. "You were thirsty that's for sure' 'She said. "I'll show you your room and where the bathroom is" Becky said. John followed Beck's up the stairs, she showed him his room and the bathroom "ok thanks Beck's I'll just finish my beer downstairs and then I'll go to bed". "It's late so I'm going to bed now, I've shown you your room, you finish your beer Johnny". "ok" John replied. Becky headed for bed. John stayed up a little longer and finished his beer. He made a fuss of the dogs and then went to bed.

Chapter 33

◆●◆

John was up early the next morning, he walked towards the bathroom, "Morning Johnny" Becky said "Morning Beck's" He replied peering around an opened door, he could see Becky sat behind a computer. "I've made some coffee in the kitchen" she said. "Thanks Beck's" John said as he opened the bathroom door. He showered, dressed, and went downstairs poured himself a coffee and sat round the kitchen table. Becky followed shortly after, "I must go to college and do a few things, would you like to come along Johnny" Becky said casually. "Love to Beck's" John said eagerly. They drove down the highway, turned off and into the college grounds. Parking up they both got out and John walked along side Beck's into the main building. They went up to the second floor in a lift, along the corridor and then Becky stopped and unlocked a door. "This is my office Johnny" She said. John sat down while Becky sat at her computer typing something for about ten minutes then said "that's it Johnny, we can go now" she paused "oh I need to get a few things from the store" with a thoughtful look on her face. John got up and followed her out the office and out the main entrance. Becky sat in the 4x4 and said "you've forgotten haven't you Johnny" smiling at him. John showed her a blank look not knowing what she was talking about. "Here's your winnings Johnny I took the $25.00 out so I owe you $475.00 here you are, handing it to him. John was really pleased and took the money and thanked her, they shopped in a big store John bought some beer. Becks said she would take him to the yacht club tonight. John was looking forward to that, not knowing what to expect.

They got back to Beck's house, Becky cooked some food and then they freshened up. It was around 6pm. "Were go now cause the ferry shuts at 10pm." Ferry John thought were going on a ferry. "How long does it take to cross" John said. "Your see" said Beck's. They got to the ferry alright; they were behind 2 cars, that's how many cars the ferry could take at one time. They watched it cross the river and return with 2 other cars, and then it was their turn. they got to the yacht club, parked, got out and Beck's said I'll show you my boat first Johnny. They walked towards what looked like a huge hanger over the water, as they got closer John could see the rows of boats each side of a wooden walkway. They passed about 4 boats on both sides and then Becks pointed. "Here she is Johnny" still pointing and looking at John. "wow that's some boat Beck's" John said staring at the boat," That's a big boat" John was still staring in disbelief. "were take her out tomorrow and do a bit of fishing" she said, "ok" said John. John followed Becky back to the club house they had a few beers, Becky introduced John to some of her friends, who were interested in John speaking English they thought his accent was awesome, she looked at the time and said " We best make a move Johnny' 'Finishing her bottle of beer. John hadn't realized the time; they'd been there a couple of hours.

It was Saturday morning; Beck's said she would introduce John to the guy who rented the granny annex on the side of her house. He was due back, any time today, John heard a car pull up outside and wondered who it was. He was sat in the kitchen drinking coffee; Becky went and opened the front door and said something to him and walked back into the kitchen. The guy followed, John stood up and shook his hand "I'm Alan and you must be Johnny" He said. "That's right" John replied.

Alan had a southern accent well that's what John thought. "Do ya like fishing' 'Alan said to John. "I love fishing on the beach or in a boat doesn't matter to me." "Well Becky we could all go' 'said Alan, Becky nodded. I'll introduce you to some friends of mine, see ya later" And he disappeared out the front door.

Just over an hour later, Alan introduced John to his friends who had turned up, "This is Steve and his stepdaughter Beth" said Alan. John shook their hands. We all got in the 4x4, Beck's was driving, we headed over to the yacht club. We were on the boat in no time, Steve and Alan had to help John get on the boat, each of them holding one of John's arms to steady him. The boat had two V8 engines Becky let her go when we got out so far, you could feel the power. John was sat on a fold up chair at the back of the boat, he could feel the power as the boat sliced through the water. Becks slowed down "This is as good as any" She said turning off the engine's. Alan got organized with the rods and baited up each one, handing one to John. The sun was hot, "Johnny" Beck's said. "Here" She said putting a blanket over John's legs. She pointed at the sun. "Your burn Johnny if you're not careful" She said with a caring look on her face, "Thanks Beck's" said John. They sat out for a couple of hours, rods at the ready, chatting and drinking beer, not one had a bite. "Let's rap it up guy's" Beck's said. Alan took John's rod and reeled it in for him. They got back and moored up, Alan and Steve tying the boat securely. We got back to Becky's and had a BBQ out the back on the decking, Becky cooked some sausages, burgers, and chicken. All washed down with cans of beer, John insisted on pouring his beer into a glass, that Becky took out of a kitchen cupboard the night before. They all thought it was funny to use a glass. Steve and Alan joked and laughed about it with John. It was getting dark, and Becky said she's going to hit the hay. Alan turned the radio on, that was in the kitchen leaving the large sliding glass door open, there were two Bluetooth speakers Alan brought out and placed them on the decking. We all sat chatting and having a laugh, about not catching anything, not even a bite. John showed them his right foot the two middle toes caught the sun. They were red and sore, he left them exposed not realizing. Alan said "your lucky Beck's gave you that blanket Johnny; else you'd have burned both legs. They had a few more laughs washed down with beer, and then decided to crash.

John was up at a reasonable time the next morning, peering around the small room where Beck's was on her computer as usual. "Morning Beck's" He said. "Hi Johnny" said Beck's preoccupied with something on the screen. John showered and dressed and sat in the kitchen drinking a black coffee. It wasn't long before Beck's appeared, topping up her coffee from the jug on the hot plate. "What about going to Washington DC Johnny" Beck's said. "Sure, that sounds like a good idea, how far is it" John replied. "It's not very far, were head out soon, got to stop for some gas first" said Beck's. "No problem, Beck's just let me know when your ready to go" John replied enthusiastically.

They both got in the 4 x 4 and headed for Washington DC, stopping on the way for gas as Beck's called it. It took over two hours, which Beck's took in her stride. As we drove through the streets Becky pointed to her right. "There's the white house Johnny". John turned his head "wow it's a big place, can we stop so I can take a picture" John replied all excited. "OK" Beck's said as she pulled over to one of the entrances, there were three police motor bikes park in a row and two 4x4 police trucks. The five policemen were chatting, as John got closer to them, he asked if Becky could take a picture, they agreed. When John stood next to them, he realized how big these guys were, He thought I'm six feet, these guys were a hell of a lot taller and armed. while Becky took a picture John shook the hand of one of them and thanked them all.

John said to Becky "Can we stop somewhere, where I could buy a hot dog from one of those mobile stands Beck's" "Sure Johnny" She said. "Thanks Beck's, one more thing, what's the DC stand for"? "That's District of Columbia Johnny, I was waiting for you to ask me that. 'she smirked looking at him, John grinned back at her.

"Where are we heading now". John said with a puzzled look on his face. "Your see" Becky replied. She parked the 4x4 and they both got out, all you could see was acres of clean-cut green grass, like a huge lawn and thousands of white crosses equally spaced apart in row's. They walked along a pathway amongst the crosses. "Johnny this is the young men that lost their lives fighting in Vietnam' 'Beck's said as they carried on walking. John was silent in ore of his surroundings. Becks suddenly stopped and walked over to one cross; John stood still, not saying a word. He watched Beck's bend down in front of one of the crosses. She stood up after a couple of minutes and walked back to John. "Johnny the name on that cross was a guy I went to school with". John didn't know what to say and felt awkward. Becky noticed and broke the ice. "Let's head back". John could feel that Becky was upset as they got in the 4x4, they both said nothing until they were on the highway.

They did stop in Washington where John bought a hot dog with onions cover in mustard, He enjoyed it. Driving back they stopped at a petrol station or gas station, as Becky would say, and John bought some beers and a lottery ticket, they got back to Beck's place late afternoon.

Chapter 34

◆•●•◆

John and Beck's walked through the house and out the back and there was Alan Steve and Beth sitting around the table on the decking Alan and Steve drinking beer and smoking. "Hi Johnny" said Alan. Steve and Beth put their hands up to acknowledge John and Beck's. "Are you guy's hungry" said Beck's." They all looked up eagerly and smiling. Becky was carrying a thick plastic bag, she must have got out the back of the 4x4 and what ever was inside was moving about, she put the bag down next to the Bar B Que turned on the gas and got Alan to half fill a large saucepan with water from the kitchen. Alan placed the saucepan on the gas stove outside. Becky and John were handed a beer, obviously Alan made a point of pouring John's beer into a glass with a huge grin on his face. John saw the funny side, grinning back. Steve picked up on it and said

"Hay Johnny come sit down with your glass of beer" sniggering like a teenager. They all had a laugh even Becks smiled. The water soon boiled, that's when Becky got Alan to empty the contents of the plastic bag into the saucepan. It was two or three dozen crabs falling into the pan. Steve and Beth were handed some news papers by Beck's, they spread them all over the table completely covering it. Becks returned from the kitchen again with a huge kitchen roll she placed on the table with two, what looked to be nut crackers. Not long after, Alan put the cooked crabs on a big plate and placed it in the centre of the table. They all dug in accept John, not quite knowing what to do. Alan stood up and stood along side John and showed him what to do or how to take the crab apart, he lifted the shell and showed John the insides, pointing with his finger, "You don't eat that part Johnny, we call it the Devil's fingers, it poisonous"? "ok" John replied. It wasn't long before the plate and around the table was full of broken up crab shell's and claw's with quite a few empty cans of beer. John was just washing down the last mouthful of crab meat with his glass of beer. Alan got up and walked over to this big plastic cooler open the lid and turned to John' 'Do you want another beer Johnny' 'he said. "Yes please" John replied. "Do you want me to pour it for you" said Alan grinning smugly. "NO, I can manage thanks" John replied grinning, knowing he was taking the mick. Steve heard and laughed, Beth was quiet, sipping on a can of coke.

It was getting late, yet again, Becky went inside but Steve, Alan and John sat around the table laughing and joking about the days events they all had and carried on drinking beer. Beth had crashed out in the RV, Steve her stepdad and she arrived in. Alan said "we know you like live music Johnny, do you want to go and see some tomorrow afternoon" Steve stepped in "it's an all-night festival outside what do ya say Johnny." "Ok" said John a bit skeptical about the all night bit?

Alan said "were stay till late and then come back ok" Looking at John "That would be great guy's" John replied looking relieved.

The next day, Becky was up early as usual on her PC, in the small bedroom with the door open, next to John's room. "Hi Beck's" said John peering in and then headed for the bathroom "Morning Johnny" He heard Beck's say. After showering and getting dressed John made his way down the stairs and into the kitchen, he sat in the kitchen drinking a black coffee as usual, his mind wondered about today's events, live music outside, I can't wait he thought. Becky appeared "Can I get you a coffee Beck's" said John. "Sure" Becks replied. "I have some errands to run". Sipping her coffee, John just gave her, "I hear your going to a music festival Johnny" "That's right I can't wait, really looking forward to it." Beck's shouted as she walked towards the front door. "Well, you have a good time, and I'll see you later alligator" and shut the door behind her.

Alan appeared saying "are you ready Johnny" John nodded, they all climbed into the 4x4.

Heading out on the highway, they stopped at a garage or gas station, Alan filled up. Steve Beth and John went inside and bought some beer's and half a dozen cokes for Beth. Steve opened the lid of this machine outside, which held bags of ice, bought 3 big bags, brought them over to the back of the truck opened the lid of the big cooler, open the bags and all the ice spilled into the box. Then he placed all are beer's in and amongst the ice.

About 45 minutes down the highway, then we turned off, onto a main road then turned again and went off road down a track and into the woods to a large clearing, where there were two stages. One large main stage and one smaller, there were quite a few people there and more were arriving. They were stopped at what looked like a check point, these women spoke to Alan the middle aged women looked at John and said "where do you come from". John replied "The united kingdom" "really cool' 'she said with a smile, waving us on. they parked up, John was getting excited with all the people and commotion all around him. They got out the 4x4, Alan reached in the back and pulled out a canvas bag. John thought a tent, Steve carrying smaller bags, which turned out to be fold up chairs for the four of them. Alan said "Stand back Johnny" He pulled a chord on the compacted mass of aluminum and canvas that was all folded up together, instantly grew into a gazebo, as if by magic. They soon settled in, sitting around the cooler full of beer under the gazebo. "Beer Johnny' 'said Alan "please' John replied. "Your have to drink it from the can this time Johnny" said Steve grinning.

They were all chatting away and suddenly there was music,

coming from the small stage.

It sounded a bit like the blues, John couldn't quite make it out, but it sounded good, John thought. The afternoon turned into night, it was still light, and Alan took John over to the main stage. There was about 4 or 500 people there so we stood at the back. The band was a Kiss tribute act, all made up with make up and costumes. The singer kicked a beach ball out into the crowd, which the crowd were punching it into the air, and it bounced all round the crowd, It was a great friendly atmosphere. As John and Alan walked back to their chairs, Beth came over and said to John "do you want to meet the band you liked that were on the small stage earlier". "Ya sure". John replied. They all sat back down under the gazebo, grabbing a beer from Steve. The 4 band members came up to John, who stood up, "Hi guy's your very good" said John shaking their hands. "Thanks, where are you from" one of them said noticing a different accent. "I'm from the UK" said John. "Wow that's along way to come to see the rock fest. 'Smirking. They all laughed. "Wouldn't mind taking home, one of those T Shirts your wearing, where did you get It., He paused. "what's it say"? said John.

The guy pulled out his T shirt from the bottom with his hands, looking down and read, "All day and all night 26th annual June Jam Rocking for a reason." The guy said "Looking at John 'I'll go back to the van and put another T shirt on, and you can have this one, were about the same size, what do you say"? John was speechless. "Thank you very much I appreciate it thank you" said John. Shortly after, the guy came back with the T shirt all rolled up and handed it to John and said "you might want to give it a wash first" they all laughed and John shook his hand again saying "thanks again" as he walked away, he turned and said "Have a good one guy's 'putting his hand up with a slight wave as he walked away.

It was starting to get dark, Alan and Steve started loading the truck, "You sit and finish your beer Johnny' 'Alan said folding his chair up. They put the bag of empty cans in the back of the 4x4, John had finished his beer and stood up. "You sit in Johnny were clear up" said Alan. They got back to Beck's place about 11.45 pm, the boys unloaded the thing's from the truck. Beth crashed in the RV saying 'good night to everybody, Steve Alan and John sat on the decking around the back and had a beer before they all crashed out.

Chapter 35

—◆●◆—

The next day John was sitting out the back, on the decking drinking a coke. When he noticed a young woman riding out of the stables on Beck's horse TJ that's not Beck's he thought. Who ever it was gave John a wave, he waved back trying to make out who she was? He was uncertain, not knowing who this person was. He suddenly remembered, Beck's saying about a young woman comes over to ride the horses to exercise them. She rode around the field for awhile then lead TJ back to the stable, awhile longer she came out and walked towards John. "Hi, I'm Sue you must be Johnny from the UK" She held her hand out with a smile, John stood up and shook her hand and said " That's me" grinning to himself. "Where's Becky" she said. "She had to go to a meeting at the yacht club" John replied. "Oh well I've got to run see ya soon, nice meeting you Johnny" she said smiling. "Hay nice meeting you to" John replied.

It wasn't long before Beck's returned, "Hi" let's go to Ocean city" She said as if on a mission. They both jumped in the 4x4, and made their way down the highway; it wasn't long before they were driving along Ocean City front. John noticed there were lots of big kites on the beach anchored to concrete blocks. A giant pink pig a black and white cat and a giant eagle. There were a lot of smaller kites to, they parked up. John followed Beck's towards the beach, then on to a pier, walking out over the sea to the end. Right at the end of the pier was a bar, half circle, John thought this is cool. "Do you want a beer Johnny" Beck's said. "Yes please, thanks Beck's" John replied. They sat at the bar, drank their bottles of beer. "You ready to go" Beck's said. John nodded as he stood up. On the way back Becky pulled over and parked next to this building, John could see it was a shop or store as Beck's called it. "Let's have a look round Johnny" She said. They got inside and John noticed the items for sale were second hand, then he notice the word antique on the wall. Beck's was talking to the owner; John walked around and saw a wooden barrel with the top off and full of walking sticks. He pulled out one or two then went for one, he took a closer look as he took it out and tried it for size. Just right he thought, the handle was metal, of a dog's head, it looked like one of Becky's dog's Slick Willie. And that's when John decided to buy it. He showed Beck's in the store, who smiled and then he handed it to the guy behind the counter. They both got back in the 4x4 and took off down the highway, Beck's said "That stick looks cool and it does look like Slick", "That's what I'm going to call it, Slick Willie" John replied quite chuffed with himself. Becks turned and looked at John and smirked. "Hay do fancy some sweet corn later Johnny" Beck's said. "Ok" John replied. They got back in the middle of the afternoon, after stopping at a farm to pick up some sweet corn. "Need the front yard grass cut "said Beck's. John chirped up "I'll do it" he said knowing Beck's had a ride on mower, like a little tractor. "Ok Johnny" Beck's said. I don't think John realized how big the front yard was; well not until he started cutting it. There were 8 established fir trees dotted about, that's how big it was. He started on the outside and worked his way in, halfway around; Alan was standing there with his arm out holding a beer. When John was due to pass him, he grabbed the beer saying "Cheer's." with a big grin on his face, then taking a mouthful of beer. The sun was still out, and John was feeling the heat, but stuck at it, till he finished. He sat down with the others, on the decking around the back. after parking the mower around the side of the house. They were all having a laugh and a joke, drinking beer, Beth on coke, giggling about something.

John put his empty bottle of beer in this recycle bin, by the side of the decking. Alan handed him another beer. "Oh, sorry Johnny, I'll get you your glass" He stood up and went inside and reappeared with John's glass. "You ok pouring it" Alan said trying to keep a straight face. "I can handle it thanks" John replied trying not to laugh.

Becky was busy with the sweetcorn, Alan went over to give her a hand, passing her a beer. Becks looked over at John and said "Thanks Johnny" John looked confused. "The front yard Johnny" said Beck's. "O of course sorry I was miles away must be the heat" replied John looking a bit vacant.

They tucked into the sweetcorn, all washed down with more beer, all laughing and joking. John looked around at his friends and thought, this is nice. Never had he been so content and comfortable with people, for such along time, than as he was then. Thing's carried on; Alan let his dog out a blonde shaggy haired mongrel called buddy. Alan would throw a tennis ball into the woods beyond the field where Sue and Beck's would ride and exercise the horses. It was pitch black, bar a couple of lights on the side of the house where we were sitting. Buddy would wait until Alan said go Buddy, and off he went right in the thick woodland. He'd find the ball and return it to Alan only Alan would throw it back into the woods again. Buddy would wait for Alan's command, "Go Buddy" Alan said enthusiastically. Buddy would jump the fence over to the woodland and disappear in the darkness. We could hear him barking, telling us he had found the ball and was on his way back. John was amazed a dog could do that, while he made a fuss of Buddy ruffling his hair up on his head. John thought to himself I'm never going to forget this trip. Alan said " help yourself Johnny" pointing to the cooler full of beer.

Becks had gone in, Beth said good night and crashed in the RV, Alan put Buddy back in his kennel. John got another beer, all three sat there talking about the rock festival and the kiss tribute band. They all agreed they had a great time, John thanked Alan and Steve yet again. "Hay Johnny were glad you had a good time" said Alan. Steve said "I'm hitting the hay" John and Alan agreed.

Chapter 36

◆◆●◆◆

John and Becky were in the 4x4 and down the highway the next morning, it was about forty minutes and they turned off and ended up at this farm growing all sorts of plants in green houses. They both got out, John followed Becky towards one of the green houses which were huge. They looked around inside, Becky seemed to know what she was looking for, from behind a young girl came up to us and said, "Hi can I help you guy's" with a lovely smile. Becky and the young girl conversed for a few minutes as John stayed back, then they both went further into the green house, John could see the girl pointing at different plants. John went and stood outside where it was cooler in the shade. Becky followed the girl further IN. They eventually reappeared, the young girl wheeling half a dozen trays of plants in a wheelbarrow. The girl loaded the plants in the back of Becky 4x4 "Ok thanks very much" said Becky walking back to the 4x4, after paying for the plants in the office. The young girl said "have a nice day" putting her hand in the air and waving as she walked away.

"Are you hungry Johnny" Beck's said as they pulled away. "Just a little" John replied. "We can stop at a diner on the way back, for a coffee and pan cakes or something, how does that sound". John raised his eye browse and nodded "okay" he said excitedly. They travelled down the highway for a few miles then Beck's turned off, driving along the road, and pulling into this car park. After parking the car, John followed Beck's into the diner, it was just like out of the movies. Unbelievable he thought as he looked around, then sat down with Beck's on the other side of the table. They both picked up and looked at a menu, "what are you having Johnny" Beck's said. "OH, not sure" He paused reading the menu. "Oh, I'll have egg on toast and a black coffee Beck's, what are you having" John asked. "I think I'll have the same with grits" Becky said rubbing her chin with her finger's and still looking at the menu. The waitress came over and said "Hi my name's Jill can I take your order". She said in a soft tone. Becks gave her both their orders; the waitress asked John what kind of bread would you like, what kind of coffee would you like, reeling of a load of different types of bread then coffee. "How would you like your egg" The waitress said. John just said the first thing that entered his head "over easy please but no grits thanks" John said while watching the waitress write it all down. "So, what do you think of the good old USA Johnny"?

Said Becks, when the waitress left to get their coffees. "I love it Beck's it's so different compared to the UK, the people here have a totally different out look or perspective in life, which is good, and they are truly happy if someone succeeds in life and They pat them on the back so to speak and are truly happy for them. It's a bit different in the UK" John said showing a slight smile. "We all look at thing's differently Johnny, we all put are own spin on thing's throughout are life's" said Becky being very philosophical, John nodded as he saw the waitress getting closer. She served the coffees, then returned with the eggs on toast, and Becky's grits. "Why don't you try some Johnny" said Beck's pointing with her knife at the grits, that were in a little dish, on the side of her plate. "I don't think I can Beck's it doesn't look very appetising to me, I think I'll just stick to egg on toast thanks". Becks looked at John then shook her head and rolled her eye's smiling and then started to cut into her egg on toast.

Becky was just finishing her coffee when John said. "What is grits" looking a bit bewildered. "Grits" she paused. "Johnny grits is like porridge, it's boiled corn mill" She replied surprised he didn't know that. " Oh" thanks". John replied looking relieved with the answer.

Becks called the waitress over for the check, she paid cash leaving a tip on the table.

We drove on back to Beck's place, on the way there, she got a call on her mobile. She answered with the hands free, a voice said "Hi Mum". "Patrick" She replied. "I'm on my way home I've borrowed a friend's bike " He said. "Ok son" Becky replied.

She hung up and took a deep breath raising her shoulders then letting the air out, as if she had just sat in a truck. She looked at John and said "That was my youngest son, your meet him later." She looked as if a great weight had been taken off her shoulders.

They got home to Beck's place; Steve and Beth were packing up their things in the RV. John wondered over, 'Are you going guys?" John said. "I've got to get back to work Johnny and Beth is due back in school Monday, she's going on to college, to do nursing." "That's great" said John. "It was nice to meet you guy's" John said a bit disappointed they were leaving. "Hay it was nice to meet you to Johnny" said Steve. Beth got out of the RV and shook John's hand then decided to hug him. "You have a safe trip home to Johnny' 'said Steve. "Drive safely guy's" John said as he turned and walked towards the front door and went inside the house. He walked towards the kitchen where he could hear somebody, Beck's was there sat drinking coffee. "Coffee Johnny, I've just made it?" She spoke. "Yes please" John replied watching Beck's get up and grab a mug from the cupboard and poured him a coffee. They sat there for awhile, "Beck's could you check this lottery ticket for me" said John as he looked in his wallet and pulled out his ticket. "Sure" said Beck's. "I'll check it later" she replied. "Ok thanks" said John.

Steve and Beth were ready to leave, Alan left work early to say goodbye, we all stood on the drive as they left, all three of us were waving and shouting see ya, have a safe trip. Beth stuck her head out the window shouting "Bye"? They took off in the direction of the highway.

As we turned to go in, Becky said "Do you want to go to a bar tonight, Johnny, I have some friends playing there." "I'd love to" John said all excited, "what kind of stuff do they play' 'he said. "Hay that's a surprise Johnny" she replied with a grin on her face. John looked a bit lost but said nothing, he was excited they were going to see some more live music.

Patrick arrived a little later that day, pulling up outside on a red full fairing bike Beck's introduced John to Patrick, they shook hands, "Nice bike" John said having had a look earlier. Patrick replied "ya it's pretty cool I've borrowed it from a friend it's a Yamaha 850cc." "Wow" John said. Patrick turned to his mother to say he was going to a party tonight and drop the bike off there and might be late getting back. Beck's nodded to say ok, sipping her coffee.

John was up stairs freshening up when Beck's said "Are you ready Johnny" standing at the bottom of the stairs, looking up. "one minute" he replied, opening the bathroom door they jumped in the 4x4 Alan got in the back, John not realizing he was going to, more the merrier he thought. They drove into town, turned right at the lights into a car park. They stopped outside this big building and went inside, it was something John had never seen before, the bar was in the middle a circular shaped bar, there were 4 girls behind the bar serving. At the far end was a stage with a set of drums, bass guitar and a electric guitar on it. John was getting excited he couldn't wait for the band to start, and where were they he thought. Anyway, he soon forgot that when Beck's said "Lets sit over there' 'As she pointed, John followed her. Alan stood at the bar and ordered 2 bottles and a glass of beer for John. He brought them over, placing them on the table, handing Beck's a bottle first, then putting the glass of beer in front of John "There you go Johnny, one glass of beer" still grinning John smirked and took a sip. It wasn't long before the band started, by that time the place had filled up. Great atmosphere and noisy, with cheers and whistles after each song. They started the next number, John thought I recognize that song" He paused for thought. "It's the Beatles, Get back" he said to himself. They had a good night. Alan spotted some friends of his at the bar, and went over for a chat, he returned a little later with some beers. Thanks Alan John said picking up the glass of beer from the table and taking a mouthful. Beck's leaned towards John to say "Are you enjoying it Johnny" she said knowing the answer already. "This is great Beck's I'm having a great time; it was all worth it, the 7 hours or more flying over here and everything, never thought it would be this good, but I've had a great time, thank you very much." looking at Beck's with a big grin on his face. "You're welcome my friend from across the pond" She looked at John and showed a little smile then turned to watch the band. The night was coming to an end, the crowd were wild, shouting and whistling for more and Beck's said "drink up Johnny" John finished his beer and followed Beck's out. Alan appeared as they got in the 4x4 they got home, Beck's went to bed, John followed Alan out the back on the decking, it was still warm even at that time of night and had a few beers before crashing out.

Chapter 37

◆◆ ● ◆◆

John was up the next morning, he thought; get straight in the shower, dress, and downstairs for a fresh black coffee. Being preoccupied with his thoughts he walked right passed the room where Beck's was checking her emails and stuff. He opened the bathroom door as there were no lock on it, he suddenly heard a scream in all the mist from the shower. "Sorry, sorry" John said, he could just see a young girl in her twenties with a towel around her middle. He shut the door all disconcerted wondering what had just happened, "Johnny" Beck's said "I was going to tell you Patrick brought a friend back last night." She laughed. John could hear her, he laughed to himself, still embarrassed.

Eventually he showered dressed and went downstairs where Patrick and his lady friend were drinking coffee sat around the kitchen table. "Hi Johnny, this is Liz, you met earlier" with a grin on his face. "I'm so sorry about that" John said. " Don't worry about it" She said confidently smiling. Patrick poured John a coffee and placed it in front of him on the table, "thank you" said John still embarrassed. "What have you got planned for today Johnny' 'Pat said. "I've no idea what your mothers planned for today I'll have to wait and see" John replied sipping his coffee. "Well Liz and I got to run, were meeting up with some friends in town" Pat replied looking at John. "Later" they both said as they both stood up and walked out the kitchen down the hall to the front door. "Later" John replied watching them leave.

A few minutes later Beck's appeared "Pat and his friend have gone have they" she said. "Only just" John replied. "I know you like motorcycles Johnny, so I thought we could visit the local HD Centre, what do you say" Beck's said casually. "That would be awesome" John replied. Having heard that word a lot while he's been there so he decided to put it in his vocabulary. "Ok let's go Johnny" said Beck's.

They hit the highway and 25 minutes later they pulled up outside the HD Centre. There was a big sign on the roof it said Harley Davidson. John was excited and couldn't wait to get inside. He opened the door for Beck's then walked inside to see bran new immaculate bike's so shiny, gleaming polished stainless steel and that bran new smell in the air. There was even a trike in light blue, John didn't look at the prices he was only interested in the bikes. He knew he would never be able to ride one, but he had so much admiration for the name, it was nice to see such spectacular engineering he thought. Before they left john bought a couple of Harley T shirts a coffee mug and a base ball cap.

On the way back John asked Beck's if he could use her computer, "Sure Johnny" she said with no hesitation. "If you want to create your own account then delete it before you go' 'she said. "Ok thanks Beck's" John replied.

When they got back, John went straight on Beck's PC, created an account then began to Email the travel agent he booked the trip with. Pointing out the fact that there was no help at Heathrow or Philadelphia airport to assist him. He also said that he was discussed that he had to struggle with his case and shoulder bag at both airports. He also said that he was going to put a formal complaint into the boss of the travel agent. Finishing with kind regards, please reply A.S.A.P thank you... That alt to do it he thought. The next day in the afternoon John thought he would check his emails. And low and be hold there it was, the reply from the travel agent. They profusely apologized and said that they have notified both airports, and on your return, trip will be a lot more enjoyable. Well, let's wait and see John thought, it couldn't be any worse than when I started this trip.

John walked into the kitchen, Beck's said "I'm fixing a sandwich, do you want one Johnny"
looking at him with a little smile. "Yes please" said John " I'm starving" he said. "Well, this will keep you going; I thought we

could eat at the yacht club tonight." Becks replied.

"That sounds great" said John, tucking into the sandwich she had just put in front of him. "This is good" John said, Becks smiled.

Later that day Beck's said " That ticket you gave me to check" John had forgotten all about it, Beck's said "that lottery ticket Johnny, you had one number that's all" John realized what she meant, showing disappointment on his face. "Well, it was worth a try" he said. They both got them self's ready and headed out to the yacht club. They pulled up outside the club and went in. Beck's put her hand up to acknowledge different people and then stood at the bar. John stood next to her and said. "I'll get these Beck's" and ordered 2 bottles of beer. They went and sat down, one of the barmaids came over with a pen and note pad to take their order, Beck's ordered a chicken salad. "What would you like Johnny" as Becky turned to look at him. "Could I have a cheese burger and chips please.''? With a hungry look in his eyes. The barmaid said "how would you like your burger" John a little confused has he had never been asked how do you want your burger in his life. "Oh, medium please" he replied trying to look self assured. She took the order and disappeared in the kitchen. "I love those American flags hanging off the walls Beck's" John said pointing at them. "There for next months celebrations the 4th of July Johnny, the day of independents from your country." "really" John said "Yes really Johnny" Beck's replied

It wasn't long before the food arrived. John looked at the plate of food and said to Beck's, "They've put crisps on the side of my plate, I asked for chips" John said all bewildered. "Johnny" Beck's said laughing. "Chips here in the states are what you call crisps in the UK." She carried on laughing. "never mind, do you want to change it" she said. "No, its ok it's my fault anyway" He laughed. After 20 minutes John said "That was the best burger, I've ever eaten" wiping his mouth with a napkin and looking at Beck's, who had just finished her salad. "Awesome" Beck's said. John replied "Awesome that's the word" and started to laugh. They both finished their beer's, Beck's got up turned to John and said "We better head back soon Johnny." John finished his beer and stood up as Beck's returned, they said their goodbyes, and one waitress had taken a shine to John and came around and gave him a hug and kissed him on the cheek. "Have a safe trip" she said sincerely. "Thanks" He replied turning and putting his hand in the air and waving to say goodbye. She waved back half heartily wanting him to stay. On the way back Beck's said "Were have to leave early tomorrow morning to get to the airport." "Ok Beck's I'll have a beer with Alan out the back and say goodbye, then I'll go to bed". "Cool" she replied.

The day had arrived both John and Beck's were showered, dressed and John was all packed and ready, he put his case and shoulder bag and not forgetting his walking stick he named slick Willie on the bed. Both were sat at the kitchen table drinking black coffee, "were have to make a move soon Johnny" said Beck's. "Ok how long does it take, again, I forgot" John said. "It's a two-and-a-half-hour drive, she said as if it were a short trip. "Plus we've got to be there two hours before your flight". Beck's said "I'll help you with your case, you carry your shoulder bag downstairs Johnny" she said, getting thing's organized. They put the case and shoulder bag on the back seat. Becks and John got in the 4x4 and headed for the highway. It was a long drive, john saw a pack of bikers going the other way, he counted nine Harley's. He must have dozed off, because there was a sudden jolt and John woke up to find they were there. It looked like chaos just like an ant's nest but people going this way that way every way. They got out to hear a plane taking off and other planes circling waiting to land. The place was Huge, it was more like a city, John grabbed the shoulder bag off the back seat then pulled the case out, and Becky came round and tied a bright red ribbon on the handle on the suitcase. John looked at her thinking why did you do that, Becky looked at John and said " it's to make your case stand out Johnny so it would be easier for you to find when you land. "That's awesome Beck's". John said he couldn't help saying it. They both grinned at each other and started to head for the main entrance, once inside, John could see where he had to go and stopped and turned to Beck's and said, "Thanks for everything Beck's I've had a great time really thank you very much" and then he gave her a hug, which took Beck's by surprise but realized it's what Johnny does and hugged him back. Beck's waved back at John while she was leaving, he put his hand up with a slow wave. John walked up and handed his ticket and passport to the guy behind the counter. "Thank you Sir," he said typing something in the computer. "Would you place your case their sir thank you." He put a ticket on the case and then placed it on the conveyor belt behind him. John watched his case disappear through an opening. "Ahh ok sir if you like to take a seat over there and, I'll send someone over to assist you" smiling and handing back the ticket and passport to John. "Thank you" said John.

A few minutes went by then this guy pushing a wheelchair turns up and say's. "are you needing assistance sir" John replied "Yes please" while getting in the wheelchair, John was glad of the help. "My names Benjamin sir" he said. " My names John" John replied. People seemed to move out the way when you're in a wheelchair but there was the odd one or two that didn't bother, which was so annoying, they were in their own little world. They went through customs and out the other side quickly, they were going along at a good pace when John remembered his walking stick. They didn't give it back, he panicked. " My stick I need my stick" John yelled out. "Don't worry Sir we can go back and get it" Benjamin said trying to calm John down He turned the wheelchair around and went back and John picked up slick Willie, and firmly held on to it. They got to the departure lounge, and that's where Benjamin said "This is as far as I go Sir, so if you liked to take a seat over there". gesturing by pointing with his finger. John got out of the chair and pulled out his wallet he had $8.00 and a pocket full of change left which he gave to Benjamin for doing a great job. "thank you, Sir," Benjamin said "No thank you very much"

John said with a genuine smile on his face. Benjamin said meaningfully "have a good trip Sir." "Thanks." John replied and Benjamin turned the wheelchair around and left.

John sat down and waited, it wasn't long before a guy in a uniform came over to John and said "Can I see your ticket sir" He looked at the ticket then handed it back. "If you'd like to follow me sir, I will take you to your seat, "Can I carry your bag for you" he said " Yes please" John said following him with his walking stick. John sat on the plane with the isle on his right side, so he could stretch his weak leg without getting up. He sat there thinking about all the things he had done while in the states, Becky, Alan, Steve, and Beth. I'm never going to forget it he thought, smiling to himself. He thought about all the things he had been through after the accident the turmoil, finding out about Gina and who is real friends were. He put his head back on the rest and thought to himself I've come along way since the accident. He felt a sense of pride and admiration for himself, he smiled, good for you my son he thought to himself. Before he new it, the plane started to fill up with passengers. The seats soon filled up, one woman was carrying her baby, she sat three rows in front of John, her baby was crying and making a lot of noise, but Mum soon settled her baby down. People kept boarding until the last, John heard the door being shut, and a couple of hostesses appeared. The Captain spoke over the P.A. "This is your Captain speaking wishing everybody a pleasant flight and we don't expect any bad weather or expect any problems throughout the flight thank you." He said very confidently. John sighed and felt a little more relaxed and relieved this time. The hostesses were handing out sweets before taking off, John had one and put it in his mouth straight away, The only difference this time was he knew what to expect. The plane took off, John got lightheaded, just like the first time, the sweet helped him take his mind off it, and the plane climbed and then seemed to level off. The other passengers were settling in for the flight. On the back of every seat was a screen so you could watch a film or track the flight and see how high and how fast they were going, John left that alone. He thought to himself I don't want to know that sort of information. He had the in-flight meal, which didn't taste to bad and a small bottle of beer. When he had finished, he thought, I need a leak. He got himself up and walked towards the back and used the loo, returning to his seat. Feeling quite chuffed that he stood up and felt quite relaxed, at what he had just achieved. This is going to be a lot easier, he thought. As he settled into his seat, he thought about the return trip back to his flat in the village. And he hoped Heathrow were going to look after him like they did in Philadelphia airport. He was dreading the thought of a long walk through the airport, no he thought to himself, slowly turning his head from side to side, after that Email he sent to the travel agent. He felt confident they would look after him, yeah he said to himself. Suddenly the lights went dimmer, a hostess leaned over to John and said. "If you pull the leaver on the side of your seat sir, your seat will lean back so you can have a sleep". Showing a little smile. "Ok, thank you" he said while pulling the leaver, he got himself comfortable, and slowly shut his eyes and drifted off.

Chapter 38

John woke up hearing chatting and passengers straightening up their chairs, then the lights turned from dim to normal. John rubbed his eye's and turned on the little TV screen on the back of the seat in front of him. He went through the channels and settled for a movie. He sat there not knowing how long he'd been asleep for, still sleepy, he kept on watching the movie, in between dozing off and then opening his eyes again. He woke up suddenly hearing a baby crying three rows in front, Mum stood up holding her baby, gently rocking her arms from side to side to settle her baby down again. His body clock was all over the place, as Beck's was five hours behind John in the UK. He didn't know what time it was, even what day it was, oh well he thought, when I get home, I'll soon know about it.

The hostesses were going round telling the passengers to

buckle up; John thought how long have we been flying for, it can't be much more. The Captain spoke on the P.A "This is your Captain speaking, we will be landing in approximately 20 minutes, I hope you had a pleasant flight, please fasten your seat belts, thank you. That's answered that then, John thought. It wasn't long before the plane seemed to circle and then descended, John felt the wheels hitting the runway, with a bump and slowing down rapidly before long the plane was heading off the runway and came to a halt. All the passengers were eager to get off, one of the hostesses spoke over the P.A "Please remain seated thank you" she said courteously. Everybody was talking, John had the same notion as they had, to get off the plane but he new they'd all have to wait. A hostess appeared and spoke to John " excuse me sir please would you remain seated until all the other passengers have left the plane" she said politely. "Ok" John said shrugging his shoulders as if to say no worries.

John sat there watching all the passengers grab their bags and slowly move along the isle and off the plane. A hostess gestured with her hand waving to John from the front of the plane, "It's alright to leave the plane now sir" Smiling at John. Oh, good he thought, he got up grabbed his bag and slick his stick and walked towards her and followed her out the door. He managed to grab his case off the conveyor belt. Thinking thank god Beck's tied a bright red ribbon on it or he would never have found it. As he turned a man smartly dressed said "Are you Mr. Blackmoore" "Yes that's me' 'John said. "Can I take your luggage sir."? He said pointing to what looked like one of those golfing buggies. "Yes please" John said with relief. He loaded John's case on the back seat; John sat next to his case resting his shoulder bag on his knees and holding on to Slick his stick. The man seemed to know where John needed to go, it took almost 20 minutes, with one thing and another. Then suddenly John could see an exit, they were heading towards. The man said "if you go through the glass doors and then to your left your see a row of coaches, there all parked in bays, your coach is H11". "Thank you very much" John replied and gave the guy a tip. He walked towards the coaches to H11; the driver was already loading other passengers' cases. The driver looked up at John and said. "Leave your case their sir, and you get on the bus" John said "You are going to Bridgwater Somerset aren't you" John said with a worried look. Looking at John with a red face as he strained to pick up one large case and put it in the storage compartment on the side of the coach with the other cases "Don't worry sir, that's where I'm stopping." John got on the coach, relieved, and sat the same side and near the back where the toilet was. He felt a lot more relaxed, he felt relieved in some ways, as he was going home. All the passengers were on board and the driver sat at the helm starting the engine. They were making good time getting out of Heathrow and onto the Motorway; John sipped on a bottle of water Becks had given him before they left. He heard talking and laughing, a couple of girls were giggling about something at the front. He drifted off to sleep thinking about home, well he thought to himself I've always been a home bird. Time went by and then John woke up to see they were coming off the motorway, He recognized his surroundings. They were coming into Bridgwater and a matter of ten minutes they pulled into the bus station. John could see Irene standing on the pavement looking up at him, She smiled pleased he was home safe. John got off the coach and stood and waited for the driver to pull out his case. People were everywhere hugging, kissing, shaking hands, laughing, and chatting. John was still waiting for the driver to pull out his case, there it is he said to himself. He stepped forward grabbed the case with the red ribbon on it and with his shoulder bag started to walk around the other side of the coach where Irene was.

He greeted her with a hug and a kiss on the cheek. "How was your trip" she said. "Brilliant" John replied.

"Let's get your things in the car" she said. She drove John back to his flat, where again she helped him with his case, and left it by the front door. John turned towards her and gave her a hug and a kiss, 'Thanks Irene" he said sincerely. "Your have to show me the photo's you took while you were there" she said. "I'll show you on my PC Irene give me a couple of days to sort myself out first". He said looking tired. "Give me a ring" she said standing by her car putting her hand to her ear shaped like a phone. "Will do" John replied waving as she drove off. John turned to the front door, put the key in the lock and turned it, thinking to himself, I'm home as he stepped inside.

Acknowledgement

Without the help of all the people mentioned in my dedication, I wouldn't have been able to write this book.

Printed in Great Britain
by Amazon